Patty -

Thank you ...
this dream come 7...
Cheers to your own drea...
those things that keep you
up at night, coming to pass.

Love,

Leah

CAPSHAW

CAPSHAW

MARSHAL HUNTER
LEAH SPRADLIN

NOBLE GIANT BOOKS

First edition: September 2015

Text ©2015 Marshal Hunter & Leah Spradlin

Cover design by Apollonia Hunter

Also available in Ebook.

Published by Noble Giant Books, a division of Noble Giant Films, LLC - Hampton, VA

For special discounts for bulk purchases, please contact Noble Giant Books at 757.637.0223 or info@noblegiantbooks.com

Manufactured in the United States of America

ISBN 13: 978-0692467527 (Paperback)

ISBN-10: 0692467521

To my love, my life, my very breath
-MH

To my very first character, my son Kade.
-LS

CAPSHAW

A Mystery Novel

NOBLE GIANT BOOKS

Some secrets aren't worth
the cost of knowing.

PROLOGUE

*A*cid clung to every surface and hung in the air, cloaking the inside of the squatting, wide shed in a fragile state of incomplete chemical processes. The tin walls were sagging and dented in many places, and the dirt floor was covered by ragged tarps in order to not record footprints. There was no TV calling softly in the background, no conversation, no traffic outside... just the quiet of the mountains and the *chiff-snap* of raw ingredients being unwrapped from their packaging. No one spoke because no one had anything to talk about.

A girl with flat blonde hair hanging down her back and eyes half closed stumbled on the uneven ground and toppled over a frothing container of chemicals. The acid spilled across the dilapidated table, shredding what finish was left on it and sending the acrid smell of burning polyurethane through the room. The two men nearby looked up at the smacking and fizzing and the mumbled cries of despair, stopping their work but observing from where they sat without much concern. The girl cried as she tried to clean up the mess and hide her mistake, but the rags and towels just made the smell worse.

Through the frail walls, the sound of a pickup truck coming through the woods compelled them to appear busy, and the girl to panic. Someone jumped from the bed of the truck onto the first dead leaves of autumn and crunched up to Warehouse One. A hollow-eyed young man, gaunt with malnutrition, pushed the door open and plopped a bag of coffee filters on the work table. "Git back to work," he told the others.

Outside, both truck doors slammed, and two sets of heavier and more deliberate footsteps made their way through the filthy yard, a tense conversation volleying between them. A muscular middle-aged man with a shaved head bludgeoned the door open and thundered inside, followed by an older man with gray hair sticking out from underneath his trucker's cap.

"What does he want?"

"I don't know, but you better watch out for him," the old man warned.

"He ain't gonna mess with me."

"Yeah, but..."

"I been smarter than the Sheriff's department for a long time, you know that."

"But what about..." the old man looked away. "Her?"

"I ain't worried about her," the burly man said with a

snicker.

"Yeah but you know she been over with the judge, tryna make new laws and all," the old man whined.

"Since when did the laws matter?" the burly man glared, getting annoyed.

"Well they ain't playin' around this time."

"I'm not playin' around either."

"Well I'm just sayin' is all. If she comes and finds out about all this, she ain't gonna be satisfied with sendin' you to the county jail, she's gonna…"

The big man slammed his fist against a cabinet. It moaned from the impact and hung a few degrees further away from the wall than before. The burly man spoke with a shortness of breath that belied his rage. "I don't care who she thinks she is. I don't care who's been diggin'. All I know is my Mossberg ain't runnin' from nobody. Quit telling me about what everyone else is doin' and you make sure you stay doin' yer job. You let me handle it." The older man tried to interject and got sworn at. "I'll kill anyone who gets in my way," the bald man bellowed. "I'll kill 'em, okay? They ain't gettin' away with it. Nobody's gonna get away with crossin' me." He shuddered at his own wickedness, and realized everyone in the room was still, listening. He clapped loudly and they jumped, nerves shredded, and got back to their chemistry. "Get the rest of this boxed up, they gonna be here to pick it up soon," he said, checking his watch. The burly man calmed himself by smoothing the stubble on his head and tugging his belt loops north. "Better go on down to the tavern before I'm late for my dinner."

He looked around the dank building, but no one looked back up at him. Pleased, he gripped the flimsy door handle as if to crush it like a soda can, his shoulder bulging with unnecessary force. As he whipped the door closed behind him, the wind rushed in and blew the coffee filters onto the floor, and the boy with the hollow eyes cursed at the inconvenience.

CHAPTER ONE

A stately coffee machine slept silently on the black granite counter, patiently waiting for 5:29 to expire before clicking over to 5:30 and waking up its inner cogs. A few stray rays of sun slipped through the bamboo blinds and into the kitchen, seeking out metal to ricochet from. The only sound in the apartment was the tap dance of a keyboard coming from the bedroom and the low TV volume.

Logan sat on his bed with his laptop on his lap, although he had been up all night and accomplished nothing. He drowsily ran a hand through his short dark hair and looked down next to him. His beautiful wife Sadie lay there, sleeping deeply. She was quite pregnant and eternally exhausted. Her dark hair spilled over the pillowcase, and her muted blue eyes were resting behind tired lids.

Frustrated with his lack of progress and the impatience of the sun, Logan closed his laptop and slid out of bed, dropping his weary head to his palms. He hadn't turned in a worthwhile story to his editor at the newspaper since the Fourth of July.

This was no time for his career to slow down, not with a baby on the way. Desperation crept over him the longer he sat there. He had been up early and to bed late every night for weeks, trying to find that elusive perfect story. After all the high profile articles that bore his name in the Chronicle, the newspaper business is a what-have-you-done-for-me-lately kind of job. The moment every smash hit Logan wrote was published it was time to find another one. That's what he loved about it. He summoned his inner tiger and told himself it was a new week, and a new month. Today was going to be lucky.

A segment on the early morning news caused Logan to sit up and notice, turning the volume up a bit. *A what was missing? Where?* He couldn't have heard correctly.

"…Josh Hanover has our story."

"Southwestern Virginia – the heart of the Appalachian mountains – is known for its southern charm, handmade arts and crafts, and its beautiful scenery. From the tiny towns peppered throughout the hills and hollows of coal country to the sparse handful of industrial cities, the people who call Appalachia home share a common sense of purpose and values. At least they thought they did… until the early hours of May 30, 1988."

Logan watched his TV fill up with animated photographs of a police officer and his small family. Sepia toned pictures of rural Virginia and scenes from a criminal investigation thrust themselves across the screen.

"It was in the early hours of the morning that Sheriff Thomas Capshaw, along with his wife Leanne and their 3-year-old son, mysteriously vanished from the town of Barwell, VA."

Logan gulped. His arms involuntarily broke out in goose bumps.

"The sheriff's vehicle was found floating in the nearby Carrollton River, but no bodies were inside. It appeared to have gone off the bridge, but whether that was intentional or accidental was never determined. The local police found no trace of the family, and even after involvement from major TV networks and crime scene investigation units, the whereabouts or demise of this family remain unknown.

"This year marks the Twenty-Fifth anniversary of the most confusing tragedy to ever hit this small town community... And despite years of intense scrutiny from national media outlets, the FBI, and numerous academic institutions, today we are no closer to understanding what happened on that bridge than when the accident first happened."

"Thank you, Josh. I'm Sandra Vo, reporting..."

Logan slowly pushed the OFF button on the remote. He sat motionless for a few moments. Then, suddenly snapping out of his thoughts, he smiled and boldly left the bedroom.

As steam billowed over the top of the shower curtain, fogging up the mirror, Logan quickly and vigorously rinsed soap down the drain and slammed the water off. He tried dressing quietly, but then, like a gunshot, his alarm went off.

"Babe, please…" Sadie mumbled as she rolled over.

"What do you need Sadie?" Logan asked, smirking. He was one of those husbands who enjoyed annoying his wife.

"Turn it off!" She barked, her pregnancy madness on a very short leash.

"Honey, I really don't know what you're talking about." Logan teased, knowing it would aggravate her.

"Logan I am not kidding! I will murder you if you don't turn that stupid alarm off right now!"

The young reporter finally shut off the alarm on his cell phone and walked around to her side of the bed, kneeling beside her.

"You know you love me," He said teasingly and leaned in to kiss her, but she playfully turned away. "You jumped straight to murder, just like that?" Logan asked with melodramatic seriousness.

"I did. And you know what? If I have to spend one more night listening to that excessive tapping, I might actually do it."

Logan leaned close to her belly and placed one hand on each side. "Ok… I'm sorry that my hard work has damaged your mother's brain. But let me ask you a question, my little tot... my little... nibblet. Would it make a difference if I finally found... it?"

Sadie curiously opened one eye. "Really? You finally found a story?"

Trying not to grin from ear to ear, Logan nodded. "I think so."

Sadie bounced onto her knees like she wasn't pregnant at all and threw her arms around his neck, planting a deep kiss on his lips.

The last seven months since the thrilling announcement of their first child had proven to be the most difficult time of her relationship with Logan, much in part she imagined because his career had taken a dip right after Sadie stopped working. At first, they both thought it was just an unlucky phase that the newspaper business seemed to slow down at the same time as Logan's ability to land a single story on any important page of the paper. But after Sadie's first trimester ended and the weeks started to tick by faster and faster, Logan's inner charisma and drive had seemed to wane as the pressure mounted to care for his burgeoning family. He became worried more than he was hopeful. And as much as Sadie tried to uplift him, he often became distant and cranky, shutting her out. Sadie had aimlessly wondered, many days alone at home, what would become of them and why the most joyful development a couple could seem to have, adding a baby to the family, seemed to have the opposite effect on Logan than the doting father she had always believed he would be.

As Sadie kissed her husband, all of these thoughts flooded her mind and a thousand questions besides. He pulled away, smiled tightly, and commented that the coffee was ready. Sadie sat back down on her feet, and reclined back onto the pillows. There seemed to be nothing that could keep Logan in a good mood anymore.

Stirring cream and sugar into a fresh cup of Caribou coffee, Logan looked up at the ceiling as if scrolling through the many tabs open in his brain. "So, what do you have going on today, Babe?"

"Francis is taking me to breakfast," Sadie replied from the bedroom. Logan returned with his coffee and a glass of grapefruit juice for her.

"That's nice. And then what?"

"We're going shopping. I have to find something to wear tonight. Nothing fits over this belly." Sadie clutched her stomach and sighed. She looked up at Logan and saw the confused look on his face. "Don't act like you've forgotten what tonight is."

"Francis hates shopping," Logan noted as he stretched and looked at the ceiling. "Does she even own a dress?" An alert message popped up on Logan's phone. He held it up for her to see. "How could I forget? Between you and mom, I think it's safe to say I am more than well aware." He looked down and busied himself with checking other notifications and messages.

"She's been planning their anniversary dinner for months.

It's all she talks about lately… how much she and your dad miss you. She is insanely excited about it, Logan! So I don't want to hear any excuses about having to work late or losing track of time…"

"Yep," Logan replied distractedly. A text chimed.

Logan, there is a job opening at Collings-Reed Financial. I will put in a good word with the broker there if you will send in your resume.

Dad, trying to control everything again. Logan clenched his teeth and deleted the text. His phone chimed again and he rolled his eyes.

Newspaper business is dead. There is a great market for young brokers and this firm is growing. You can't provide for your family selling news stories. It's too volatile, son. Sure your wife would agree.

Logan swore under his breath and stomped his fist.

"Look, this may be just another dinner to you, but it's important to them… and to me," Sadie clarified, getting testy again.

Logan looked up from his phone. "I know what's important to my parents, Sadie" he said sternly. "I've heard it my whole life…'family comes first; loyalty over ambition'… believe me I know, but sometimes there are other things that are important too. Ok?"

Sadie's eyes began to fill with tears as she swallowed the rest of her comments. She looked down in silence.

Logan realized his tone had triggered the hormones again. "Hey… hey. I'm sorry. I didn't mean to snap at you. You're right. There's no excuse for being late… I won't be late."

"Fine," Sadie choked.

Logan walked across the room and whipped the curtains open, flooding the room with immature sunlight. He quietly looked out the window, squinting his fierce green eyes, and she faced the other way on the bed. The lines had been blurred, and it was hard to tell anymore whether their short tempers and frequent arguments were a product of normal stress or some bigger issue just out of cognizance. They were both thinking it, but communication had shut down, and neither knew how to open it back up without sacrificing their pride. They were still for a measure of uncomfortable, thick silence. Then Logan walked past his wife and out the door, out of the house, and left for work.

Leaving his building and crossing Union Street, he noticed the glass store front of the bagel shop on the corner at Clifford Street reflected a sky full of thick, pewter clouds. The heavens loomed dark, and he could tell it was going to storm. He looked up as he walked and watched the birds struggle against the wind in their attempts to batten down the hatches. His thoughts wafted back across many years to the first storm he had ever encountered, one he had never seen anything like since.

Over a wide lake somewhere, thunder and lightning had

battled ominously in the distance throughout the day, humming with crackling force. As evening had approached, the storm had mushroomed quickly and his dad had rushed to close up the house and prepare for flooding. The crowning crescendo of the mighty forces of the weather was about to unfold. With the wonder and awe of a child learning all there is to know about the world, Logan had wandered outside toward it as if he could somehow get close enough to touch it. Then the rain had started to pour. That was when his father had run after him and scooped him up, against Logan's will, and carried him back inside despite a cacophony of wailing and thrashing. He remembered feeling like something had been stolen from him and spent the rest of the night crying in his room at the heartbreak of missing out on the storm. Even as a three-year-old, he recalled experiencing resentment toward his father for a long time. Maybe it had never gone away? It was Logan's earliest memory.

He exited the subway and hustled the two blocks to his office, the headquarters of The Chronicle. His stomach turned with frustration. As he shouldered the early morning chill, the Chicago city life blurred all over itself into a wash of meaningless rubbish; he scoffed at nothing in particular as he pushed through the rotary door under the regent emblem of the paper.

Chicago Chronicle

The building was a relic, a symbol of past greatness that was struggling to keep up with modern times. Even at twenty-seven, Logan was beginning to feel the same way.

He walked through the lobby on auto pilot. The ornate designs on the walls and doors of the lobby were all lost on him as he wandered to the elevator and waited. The atrium was as quiet as a library, with an occasional phone ringing with shrill disrespect for the utter silence. *Why don't they play music around here?* He wondered. *Music would help.*

As the doors to the 18th floor opened, the silence was punctured by the buzz of the newsroom. It was not a stiff energy, but rather a machine that had run for many years and found its smooth stride long ago. The culture of the newsroom, although the luster was fading in his mind's eye, was still intoxicating and easily carried him along with the current. Dodging between throngs of reporters, journalists, interns and managers fanned the flame of Logan's inner pilot light. Each head and shoulders he passed, uptight and scowling with urgency and self-preservation, was a gateway to hundreds of stories and anecdotes. To Logan, the newspaper business was the hub of all things that were known in the world, and a true and authentic love for the business lent itself to the philosophy that if he always pursued a story for the merit of the story itself, reputation and success would naturally follow. His pace increased as he navigated his way to the cubicle labeled "L. Anders."

Suddenly an arm was waving an article in his face and muttering above the din of the office. Logan fired a glare of poison in the direction of the arm. He was not in the mood for challenging remarks from self-righteous colleagues.

"Hey, Graves... do you smell that? What is that?" the head on the other end of the arm cried.

"I don't know Hawk, but it is delicious," said another useless head. "Mmmmm... You smell that, Anders? A3... A3..."

Cole Hawkinson and Garrett Graves. A whole new level of pointless. These were the other two staff writers in Logan's department, both highly educated boneheads that wandered around the office distracting everyone else from productive work with their lofty down talk. They had been hired the same cursed day and had made Logan's life perpetually intolerable ever since. Cole was pudgy and wide, ate everything in sight, and seemed to be made entirely of churro dough. Garrett was tall, handsome, and obsessed with his body. Everyone knew all about the previous evening's workout by the morning meeting every day, and he wouldn't permit a single idle calorie to pass his lips, nor anyone else's without chiding them with guilt. The day he had proudly shown Logan an 8x10 photo of himself flexing, slick with oil and smiling wide, had been the day Logan silently parted company with Garrett Graves.

Alexis Rojas, the well-put-together Latina intern, snatched their papers, pretended to take a whiff and grumbled with annoyance. "Smells like another day old story you clowns dug out the dumpster at the Tribune to me," she sneered. "A3 still isn't the front page! But what would I know. I'm just an intern, right?" She pushed the papers back into Cole's billowing chest and handed Logan a cup of coffee. Silenced by Alexis' spicy Spanish fury, Garrett and Cole sauntered off to annoy some other employee before getting another earful.

"Thank you Lex," Logan said, accepting the coffee and taking a sip of liquid life-purpose as black as night and as thick as beef jerky. "And thank you for that dramatic display of loyalty. What is my run down for the day?"

Alexis smacked her gum. "Ok well, Mr. Strauss has moved the pitch meeting up to 7:30, so you have 'bout fifteen minutes... but you should probably check your email first. Corporate's supposed to send out a memo today about layoffs."

"What?" Logan declared in disbelief.

"Yeah, I wouldn't waste my time prepping for a pitch meeting if I was getting canned... just saying." Alexis walked away, hips swaying proudly, leaving Logan staring ahead, dumb-founded. He knew he'd had a weak month. This could be bad.

He snapped his neck in her direction and heard himself say, "What does that mean?!"

The crowded board room was brimming with reporters, editors, and wanna-be reporters and editors. They filed in like penguins, all hoping for someone to toss them a fish. Most of them were diligently focused, but, of course, there is always that one obnoxiously loud person that can't help but annoy everyone just for their own personal enjoyment. This office had two: Garrett and Cole.

Eighty percent of the entire room was taken up by the long table and about twenty percent of the staff who were seated importantly on rollie chairs. The twenty remaining percent of square footage was left for the other eighty percent of the staff to stand and fidget.

Logan's boss, Steven Strauss, was the chief editor for the investigative columns. He, his third cigarette of the day, and his mop of musty gray hair sat at the far end of the table. The toll of the newspaper life had left a visible receipt on his face. He had dark bags under his eyes that screamed loud and clear, 'The coffee isn't enough.'

He slouched in his chair with one knee crossed over the other and a binder tottering atop it and the edge of the table. He studied the documents, making notations as the rest of the staff settled into a cramped mass. Logan was the last person to slip in, having been furiously researching the idea he was about to present. When he was ready to commence the meeting, Mr. Strauss looked over his glasses and called for everyone to pay attention.

"Alright let's get started," he said, plopping the binder onto the table and sitting forward. He pointed to Cole. "Go."

"As you already know," Cole began with artificial nobility, "there has been a string of random burglaries on the west side – fourteen little mom and pop shops, convenience stores, places like that – that have been hit over the last month or so.

The cops have security footage, several eye witness testimonies, even a partial license plate number. Not one arrest has been made. I think the public deserves to know why."

Mr. Strauss jotted notes in his binder and pointed to another reporter. "Go."

"My boyfriend Roland took me to dinner at Marino's for our one year anniversary last night," a vivacious, petite reporter said.

"Congratulations," Alexis piped up, rolling her eyes before she could continue. Logan glared at her from across the room, hoping she would hush but unable to keep from smiling at the same time.

"Thank you," the reporter smiled, missing the sarcasm. "Anyway, this restaurant is perfect. The atmosphere, the music, the candle light... so romantic. Oh and we sat on the patio, so the stars were twinkling overhead. It was the perfect night for him to propose. And he was going to propose... until the food came. A roach the size of a half dollar crawled out from under Roland's steak." The room bristled with disgust. "I'm not even joking," She went on. "The roach could have picked up the 16-ounce ribeye and carried it off to its family... it was that big. Oh, but there's more... Roland has a weak stomach. He spewed all over the table like a frickin' volcano." By that point, everyone in the room was either laughing or gagging. Except for Mr. Strauss, who was unaffected. "So yeah... this week, I want to smear them out of business."

Mr. Strauss' index finger was firmly pressed against his

lips. He scanned the room for the next pitch. "Anders, what have you got?"

Logan hesitated. He suddenly realized he had not prepared his pitch. Cole coughed "nothing" into his hand indiscreetly. Logan straightened his tie twice, and the silence grew awkward.

"Don't hang yourself, buddy; it can't be that bad of an idea," Garrett offered loudly.

Everyone laughed except Alexis and Mr. Strauss. "Logan if you have something get on with it," He said.

"Last night, I came across a story that has the potential to re-launch this paper," Logan managed, rallying his nerve. He saw Mr. Strauss set down his pen and take off his glasses. He had his full attention. "Twenty-five years ago, a young family vanished from a small town in southwestern Virginia. Just an average, ordinary family. The husband, Thomas Capshaw, had served as the local sheriff for years without incident. Never a complaint from the public, never questioned by the mayor, never even called in sick. He was basically a better version of Barney Fife. That all changed on May 30, 1988, when Capshaw responded to a domestic dispute call around midnight. The dispatcher who sent out the call said they had received several complaints from neighbors about someone screaming and carrying on. No one really knows what actually happened - but according to the police report, multiple shots were fired but no bodies were found at the scene. What happened next is what makes this case interesting." He paused for dramatic effect, taking a sip of coffee and gazing around the room to make sure everyone was listening. "Capshaw just walked off the job at 2 or 3 in the morning. Went home, picked up his wife and kid… then drove the pickup straight off a bridge." He looked around the room again as jaws dropped and eyes widened. "The accident was reported at 3:52 am. The police, rescue workers, divers, the tow truck, everyone was on the scene by 4:00."

"That's just eight minutes," Alexis mentioned.

"Exactly," Logan replied. "In a sleepy little town with limited resources and personnel, how could they get to a remote location so quickly? Something just doesn't add up." The room began to buzz with curiosity. "And get this… No one went in the water for over three hours."

"Why wouldn't they go in the water?" another reporter asked.

Logan shrugged his shoulders. "When they finally pulled the truck from the river, the bodies were missing. The windshield was shattered but intact, and all the windows were rolled up. The doors locked."

"Well, obviously they weren't in the truck to begin with," Cole chimed, trying to steal the spotlight.

"Maybe they were, maybe they weren't," Logan answered, "but either way something was definitely being covered up."

"Ok! Stop right there," Mr. Strauss commanded, leaning back in his seat. "I do know this case. I know it well. Plenty of reporters from all over the country have tried and failed to even make a dent in it. I'm talking national reporters – with more experience than anyone sitting or standing around this table."

Logan started to speak. "I believe I can…"

"Didn't you just tell me last week that your journalistic hero is Randal Norton?" The boss was making a spectacle of him.

"Yes, but…"

"Then you already know what he said about this case. He said, and I quote, 'The Capshaw Case is an unsolvable mystery'… You are no Randal Norton, Logan."

"I've never claimed to be anywhere as good as Mr. Norton. But this story is a story worth telling. All I am asking for is a chance. Give me a chance Steven…" Logan got daggers in return. "Mr. Strauss, I know I can do this."

"No… you can't. Timmons, what about you?" he ignored Logan completely and continued gathering ideas from around the room. Logan couldn't believe he had been shut down. The more ridiculous and driveling column ideas he heard pitched, the more passionate he became. Had he really stayed up all night for nothing? The injustice was intolerable.

"Hawkinson, Garcia, we'll run with your stories. I expect a final draft on my desk by the end of the week." Then he looked right at Logan. "The rest of you, finish what you've already started. Deadlines are deadlines, people."

The staff began filing out of the room. In his frustration, Logan cut the line and jerked past everyone and out the door.

He made a beeline for Mr. Strauss' office and reached the door right behind him and followed him inside, uninvited.

"No means no, Anders."

"Except when it means maybe or yes." Logan was not giving up easily. "You told us to stop at nothing. To follow a lead till there was nothing left to follow. 'Dead ends, cold trails, don't exist at this paper!' Remember that?"

"Don't twist my words," the editor said tactlessly. "I made that speech to a bunch of doe-eyed recent college grads so they'd get off their tie-dye futons and help me sell some papers. And back then you were happy to sacrifice your comfort for the chance to get paid to write. But I'm starting to think that you'd rather write nothing at all."

"Nothing could be further from the truth!" He knew how to push Logan's buttons, and Logan knew he deserved it.

"Being a pretend writer is ten times better than being an actual writer. Unfortunately, the pay sucks," Mr. Strauss replied unceremoniously.

"I think you are being unfair," Logan challenged.

"Of course you do. How many stories have you turned in over the last month? How many?"

Logan couldn't say anything. His cranky boss tossed his binder on the desk and leaned up against the edge of it, crossing his arms.

"The Capshaw case is not a story. It's a mirage. But even if it was a story, you haven't earned the right to go chase it."

Logan bristled. "You're right. I haven't been fulfilling my monthly quota of a billion fluff pieces. I do apologize for that. But four years ago when you hired me you said that I could make a real difference here. What difference have I made?"

"You were hired to write articles to sell papers," he cornered.

"Then let me do that. I am a good reporter and an even better writer when I actually have a story worth writing. This is exactly the kind of story *your* boss wants, and you know it. Give me a chance, please…"

Logan was leaning across the big desk, being as physically assertive as he could. He looked straight beyond those tired bags and deep into his boss's eyes. They were deep green eyes, so deep around the edge they were almost teal, which Logan had never noticed. Inside this tough, aggressive manifesto of male ego hid a guy with a job to deliver on, just like Logan. As big of a risk as it was for Logan to pursue this story, it was just as big of a risk for Mr. Strauss to let him. They both knew that. But Logan wouldn't let him avoid his gaze.

"Come on," Logan whispered.

Mr. Strauss finally looked away and released a long, defeated breath of air from his toxic lungs. "Fine." He caved! "One week in Virginia. That's it. And I expect a Pulitzer Prize winner on my desk the second you touch down at O'Hare. We clear?"

Logan clenched his jaw and fist pumped the air. *Yes.*

"Let me be clearer. This is your last chance. Deliver or don't bother coming back."

"Understood, sir. Thank you, sir… Thank you."

"You'll leave first thing Monday morning. Now get out of my office."

Ecstatic, Logan blazed through the doorway and around the labyrinth of cubicles back to his desk. He yanked his chair back and sat down, his right leg twitching uncontrollably. He sat for a few moments, staring blankly into open space. The sounds of his shoe shaking and bouncing on the floor made him aware that he was doing it at all, so he stopped. He shook his head as if to bully the nerves into submission. Then his sight landed on the pile of files and papers barring the use of his computer. He quickly weighed whether to work on diminishing the pile, or shoving it out of the way and continuing his research. Option two quickly won. The adrenaline from facing off with his boss and *winning* had made him drunk with hope.

CHAPTER TWO

Sadie rested at her vanity, finishing her updo with an arc of hairspray. She wore a new dress with a simple, unfussy style in a becoming shade of aubergine crepe, a luxurious fabric for a maternity garment. She rose from her seat, orbited around to the table by the door and picked up a gift wrapped in shiny silver paper before exiting the apartment.

She couldn't help feeling a sense of numbness as she took a taxi through the furtive, jostling Chicago streets. In a city of such energy and sparkle, the inner sense of rightness had leaked away slowly, ever since she learned she was pregnant. She was finally admitting to herself that it felt as if the one thing missing in her life - a baby - had suddenly stolen all the other things that were perfect. The sense of dread she had been trying to stifle made its way up her throat and clenched itself there, squeezing a tear from its duct and down her face. Riding alone to family dinners was not what she had imagined her future would hold.

The beverage napkins at their wedding five years ago had

said 'Logan & Sadie' in silver. Everyone had remarked how perfectly their names agreed with each other, how ideal their future was going to be, what lovely children they would produce. Sadie had beamed with happiness. Her fairy tale had found her.

She had met Logan at Buxton College in Ohio. They had encountered each other once a week in their mutual business class but had not spoken until the day she came to class late, flustered, and teetering on the brink of emotion. Logan had been seated at the back of the room and had the only available seat in the class next to him, which he offered to her. She had meekly accepted and silently reprimanded herself for not applying more attention to her appearance before being divinely appointed to seat herself next to the most handsome boy in school. 'I'm Sadie,' she had whispered apologetically. 'I know,' he had replied. She blushed so hard he had leaned forward in his seat to spare her the further embarrassment of thinking he had noticed.

Logan graduated with honors and a degree in finance, at the prodding of his father, and had been hired right out of school by an investment company in Chicago. Sadie finished her degree in accounting and found a job at a retail company in the city. In a whirlwind symphony of what seemed like all their dreams coming true, they had married, moved and started their careers the summer after college. But the business world failed to arrest Logan's interest. Despite his father's many pleas to stay and work his way up, to play it safe, and to follow the old school way of making a living - within the year Logan had left investing to pursue his first love: journalism. He had knocked on the door of The Chronicle, a longstanding Illinois newspaper with a muscular reputation and a vast staff, and used his rock star attitude to get a chance at showing them he could chase down a column.

His first story had been a piece about a young woman whose dream was to be a nurse. She had put herself through school, working hard and living with her brother and sister-in-law in order to pay for her education. Sadly, the day before she finally graduated nursing school she was diagnosed with a rare form of ovarian cancer. She never got the chance to work as a nurse because she was hospitalized until she passed away a few months later, being cared for by the very medical community she had worked so hard to serve within. The irony was heartbreaking, and the whole city had mourned her death. That story got Logan noticed, and he was addicted; the pace, the platform, the grind, everything about the news industry was like crack cocaine to the boy wrestling his way out of his father's shadow and into the world at the end of his fingertips.

Lately, that boy with the fire in his eyes had grown unsettled and independent, and the tone of life had grown dim with doubt. They didn't speak of it. Logan couldn't understand why the prospect of fatherhood had so unnerved him; although, to Sadie, it was painfully obvious but in no way befitting to discuss. She felt that Logan's strained relationship with his father was causing him to question whether he was predisposed to repeat all the things from his upbringing he swore he never would. She could sense that he was tortured by the idea that he could unwittingly duplicate his father's mistakes or worse… blaze an original path that would inevitably lead his unborn child to the same resentment that he had lived with for all these years. Sadie knew Logan hated his father's attempts to control him, despite the best of intentions, but she respected Logan's boundaries and loved his parents herself without reservation.

Sadie checked her lipstick and pulled herself up out of the cab, trying to feel glamorous as she made her way up the sidewalk for a special night out. She smiled as she saw the emerald green sign with her in-laws beneath it.

Rory Faye's

Rory Faye's was an old gilded supper club full of thick drapes, iron sconces, and groomed waiters, an establishment that predated all of its patrons and simply dripped with rarity and splendor. The chef was known for his creations of culinary passion and never failed to astonish his nightly audience. It was a place of magic. A small crowd was gathered by the door, hoping to get a table without reservation. Mr. and Mrs. Logan Anders, Sr. were waiting in the crisp evening air, to one side of the crowd.

Before entering they exchanged large smiles, heartfelt salutations and a moment of monologue with the unborn baby.

"I hope you haven't been waiting long," Sadie whispered, looking around for their maitre d'.

"Not at all," Mrs. Anders smiled. "We just got here. You look lovely my dear."

"Thank you, Sharon!" Sadie said, a little too excited. "But look at you, absolutely stunning. Happy Anniversary!"

Mr. Anders enjoyed his wife being complimented and grinned widely. "Where's Logan?" He asked pleasantly.

Sadie's cheeks warmed. "I am sure he will be here any minute... but why don't we wait inside. This place is notorious for giving away tables if you are a millisecond late, and just look at the line."

Her father in law held open the door. As Mrs. Anders swept past her and inside, Sadie hesitated and glanced over her shoulder to see if Logan was right behind her like he was supposed to be. Mr. Anders paused when she didn't follow. "I just want to call him real quick to make sure he's okay," she assured as she stepped back onto the street. Her father in law nodded his head and escorted his wife into the candlelit foyer. Sadie walked a few steps away and called Logan on speed dial.

"Hello?" Logan's voice answered distantly. Sadie closed her eyes with disappointment. "Please tell me you're not still at the office."

She heard Logan pause. Then a shuffle and a bang, and running footsteps. "Of course not. Already on my way," her husband said with false confidence. Sadie hung her head, and realized she couldn't see her feet past her belly anymore. She opened her mouth to answer, but realized he had already hung up.

*   *   *

Logan sprinted across the street and down the stairs to the subway, calling "Excuse me" a hundred times as he shoved aside those who had as much right to the train as he did. He crammed his fist into his pants pocket to retrieve the subway ticket, but the ticket he pulled out was crumpled and folded. He could hear the train entering the station, and panicked. He ran to the turnstile and swiped the ticket, but it wouldn't read. He smashed the metal bars as the train pulled into the station and ripped the card through the reader over and over. He watched the doors close and the train bullet away just as the green light lit up and let him through. He slapped the rear car as it sped past, his heart beat and his failure pounding in his ears. A few city dwellers more patient than he went back to reading their papers after being pulled away by the outburst. Logan didn't care. Looking at the digital schedule, he saw the next departure wasn't for another twenty-eight minutes and kicked the subterranean wall with fury. There was no choice but to wait. He'd never make it across town in rush hour by taking a cab.

He sat down on a subway bench for ten full seconds before losing patience and bounding back up to the street. Twenty-eight minutes was a lifetime to someone who can't sit still. He was feeling lucky and hailed a cab, deciding there were plenty of detours through traffic that could work some miracles and get him across town to reconcile his mistake.

*   *   *

It had been an enchanting dinner. As much as they had tried to stall in order to wait for Logan to arrive, the restaurant was bustling and very prompt. They had indulged in rich food and deep conversation, but had awkwardly avoided the subject of Logan altogether. As they rose from the table and made their way out of the restaurant, Sadie apologized again for Logan's unrepentant forgetfulness.

"Oh, sweet Sadie… thank you for a wonderful evening," Mrs. Anders cooed, brushing her daughter in laws face with her soft hand. "It has been a wonderful evening," Sadie replied. "I just wish Logan could have made it. His job can be so demanding sometimes."

"You don't need to make excuses for him," Mr. Anders interjected. "Logan is Logan. He will do what he wants to do. Always has, always will."

"And that's alright, he's our son. We will always love him," Logan's mother said as she turned to her husband. "No matter what."

"Absolutely," he told his wife. He turned to Sadie and smiled, "But I wouldn't share a single bite of my tiramisu if I were you." His wife slapped him on the arm. Sadie smiled and embraced her mother in law warmly.

"The boy needs to know there are consequences to his actions, right?" He asked Sadie as the valet pulled up with the car.

"I couldn't agree more," she replied as she gave him a

quick hug.

"Beautiful and smart," he mused to Sadie as he opened the door for his wife. "There's no doubt you are the better half of your marriage. And you can tell him I said that." He winked.

"Make sure you let me know you made it safely to Lake Tahoe," Sadie called as she backed away from the curb.

As Mr. Anders leaned out the window, he replied humorously, "We'll be fine, but you won't be if you even think of having that baby before we come back!"

"No sir, I wouldn't think of it," She said softly.

The taxi finally swung around the corner, three blocks from the restaurant, and Logan grunted that he would walk the rest of the way. He paid quickly and got out of the car and into the dusky Chicago evening. The rush of air that greeted him every time he stepped onto a city avenue still made his heart skip a beat. The moon was waking up, ready to host the night.

As he scurried down the block toward Rory Faye's, he straightened his tie and tried to compose a rebuttal to the stream of disappointment he was sure to encounter.

Just as he crossed the last crosswalk, he saw his parent's car on the opposite curb. Sadie's back was to him, but he could see the streetlight glimmer on her wine-colored dress.

Logan started to run as he saw them leaving. Sadie

watched his parents pull away, and as Logan reached her, she turned with questioning eyes to see who was touching her back.

The expression stayed but grew dark and angry when she saw him. She didn't say anything, just turned and looked after his parent's car, which said everything.

"I'm sorry, babe. I missed the train. I know you're mad, I feel terrible, honey. I'm sorry…"

She shushed Logan with her hand, still looking at the midnight blue sedan waiting at the light. Without looking at him, he heard her whisper,

"They were so gracious… they defended you. They deserve better, Logan."

He looked away and watched his parents glide away from the light, only to stop again in traffic a few yards further. He looked back at his wife and saw her flush with anger.

As Logan reached to touch her, his ears split with a huge crash. A booming wave of breaking glass and crunching metal rippled through the crowded street corners. As he turned to look, his wife started screaming. Logan saw glass twirling through the air like confetti, and looked back at her in shock as she collapsed to her knees on the pavement. He saw wild fear in her eyes. Snapping his head around to look, he saw smoke was pouring from a car smashed into something down the block.

Logan felt warm adrenaline churn through him like blood leaking internally. He ran, blindly, into the road. His parent's

Mercedes was pinned to a lamp post by a delivery truck.

He was almost to the car when it exploded, kicking him violently onto his back on the pavement. He watched his parents' car burn, sideways and helpless, as he lay in the middle of the cold Chicago street.

CHAPTER THREE

$\mathcal{T}$he morning of the funeral, Logan was at the cemetery at dawn. He was a habitual early riser, but he had barely slept any night since his parents' death. After dutifully attempting to rest, he had risen and dressed in black and left the apartment just as the sun was starting the day. The cabbie had looked at him strangely when given the destination, but asked no questions and had delivered Logan to Patterson Gardens Cemetery as he had been told. Logan walked around the tombstones slowly, some flat and staring eternally at heaven, some large and dignified with somber messages and ornate detail. The sun rose quickly and warmed the air, and eventually, Logan stopped and sat on a stone bench at the corner of four walks that intersected near the back of the property. He turned his back to the fountain and looked out over the many acres of lost years at rest.

The longer he sat there, the emptier he became. The pressure of choosing whether to pursue a career break halfway across the country or be available to his wife was a crushing decision. He knew his father would want him to stay. "Family first," he always used to implore. Logan had always felt suffocated by the expectation. He was stubborn and independent. He hated being told what to do and favored much more the rush of taking matters into his own hands. He had always challenged his parents. But now he was faced with the dichotomy of staying in town to put his wife ahead of the burn he had to advance his career, a choice which also happened to be what would have made his father happy. But the thought of playing domestic hero made him wither inside. He had a battle to fight, and Sadie was a grown woman. She was a special lady, but she couldn't catch this lynx for him. He knew he would be a dead man walking unless he could chase down a great story.

He surfaced from the haze of his thoughts and noticed the long shadow cast by the sun behind him. He let out a troubled sigh as he realized he only had his own shadow to stand in now. His jaw turned to granite, and the decision was made.

The logistics of burying two people maimed in a wreck and a fire had only left one option: closed caskets, and only a graveside service. Logan had laid eyes on his parents' faces for the last time, and it had been six months prior to the anniversary dinner he was supposed to have attended. The guilt was asphyxiating.

Several hours later, after a bland, hazy commemoration service, the time was finally upon Logan to speak something legitimate to the small gathering of local friends of the family surrounding him at the graveside. His shoulder still ached from being bullied by the explosion several days before. He stood, motionless, at the head of two matching caskets, surrounded by faceless people dressed in black. Father Andrew introduced Logan and squeezed his arm in vaporous reassurance before stepping aside for Logan to speak.

"I don't remember a whole lot about my childhood," he began. "But one of my favorite things that we did as a family was every summer renting a cabin out by a lake." He laughed without knowing why. "Without fail... it would rain the entire time we were there. And not little showers, you know...the heavens would open up and pour for hours. And Mom, she absolutely hated it. She begged him year after year to plan the trip some other time... but he never would. Once he made up his mind, nothing could ever change it." His mind closed over the scene before him, still and lifeless, and wandered to a distant memory, unfolding images from long ago. "I remember one year in particular. A big storm rolled in over the lake. It was the most magnificent thing I had ever seen." He looked out the window, in his mind's eye, across a wide lake somewhere as the reflected storm clouds rolled past. Lightning was streaking across the sky. "Any other kid would have run terrified from the window, but not me. Fearless and curious, I walked out the front door to explore this phenomenon." A gust of wind met his face as if to uphold the recollection. "My dad rushed out behind me and grabbed me, pulling me back in the house. I kicked and screamed the whole way. I don't remember if he was mad or scared or what. All I remember was how tightly he held me... when all I wanted was to get away from him, he just wouldn't let me go."

Logan softly, sacredly, placed a crimson rose on each of the caskets of his parents and felt furious tears blur his vision.

"My dad was a great man. My mother was an amazing woman. They didn't deserve to die like this."

Logan laid next to Sadie in their bed, listening to the absence of the TV, music, ambient sounds, sounds of life. It was just quiet. He could feel Sadie compassionately searching him, unable to offer adequate words. "I love you," she managed.

Logan rolled over toward her, mustering a hollow smile. "I love you too." He kissed her cheek softly, hoping she was reassured, then rolled over again and faced away. He told her goodnight, but was wide awake. Soon he heard her softly begin to cry.

As the night trudged on, Logan struggled to find a place of comfort and peace, or at least just sleep. He accomplished nothing other than watching the shadows and light shift shapes on the walls as time passed. Finally giving in to the restlessness he got up and retrieved his laptop. With no closure to his parents' sudden death, he tried to find closure for other unsolvable mysteries, and spent the rest of the night researching the long outdated case from Virginia.

The aroma of brewing coffee perfumed the air as Logan made his way out of the bedroom with a pair of shiny black dress shoes. He softly pulled a carry on bag from the top shelf of the hall closet. Sadie was asleep and it was still dark.

He stealthily gathered travel items from the bathroom and packed them. Then he made his way into the bedroom for some clothes, and pushed the door open... right as Sadie was pulling it open from the other side, half awake.

"Whoa," She said, startled. "Logan? What are you doing?"

He stiffened. He was hoping to be gone before she woke up.

"I'm being sent on assignment," Logan said firmly.

Sadie blinked. "What?"

He ignored her and strode over to the closet, pulling out items to pack. With his back to her, he began to explain.

"With everything that happened, I guess I forgot to tell you. But remember that case in Virginia I was telling you about? Well, Mr. Strauss liked my idea because he's sending me to Virginia to see what I can dig up."

"Virginia!" Sadie cried. "Do they know your parents just died?!"

"They think it will be good for me... to have a distraction."

"What about me? Did you tell them I am eight months

pregnant? The baby could come any time now, Logan."

"I'll only be gone a couple of days, a week tops." He didn't sound reassuring, even to himself.

His wife grabbed his arm and pulled him around so he couldn't avoid her eyes. "Stop, Logan. Look at me. Baby, I know you're hurting, but running away is not going to fix it!"

"Maybe not, but staying here is killing me." He zipped his carry on case shut and kissed his wife's cheek. "I'll call you when I get there."

Without looking back, he walked down the hallway and pulled a coat and scarf from the hook by the door, leaving his coffee untouched in the carafe. He heard Sadie weeping as the door shut behind him.

The mute, bearded security guard let Logan into the building, nodding with the understanding that reporters of every kind are always in a hurry. The sun was barely up and Logan resented starting this long day without a drop of caffeine. He shuffled his way to the 18th floor, and disembarked from the elevator to a silent landscape of cubicles. He would be gone before the first early bird showed up.

Rifling through his desk and shoving some notes into his carry-on, Logan felt a surge of purpose and energy the way he imagined athletes feel when they are about to walk onto the field. He snapped his fingers coyly, mentally facing off with the daunting story he was about to go figure out. He checked his email. Of the dozens of emails he had sent inquiring about the Capshaw case to whomever he could track down in Barwell, VA, there was one reply. His heart ceased beating as he clicked to open, and read:

Mr. Anders, the uselessness of your research cannot be overstated. The Capshaw Case was closed many years ago and our town would appreciate you keeping your curiosity in the big city where there is plenty to investigate, and leave Barwell alone.

Mary Harper

Clerk of Criminal Records, Carrollton County

Barwell, VA

The brash reporter stared at the computer screen. A tremulous shade of doubt accompanied him for a moment, but then he looked out over the many cubicles that dwelt here on the 18th floor, and all of the competitive colleagues that occupied them. He thought of Garrett Graves, whose self absorbed bravado could only carry him so far in life, but was reaching his stride and could dazzle the boss if Logan didn't watch out. He thought of a great many things in the instant between ticks of the grandfather clock across from the elevator. Then he gripped his carry-on with the unapologetic force of a gruff city boy, and went downstairs to hail a cab.

*   *   *

Logan sat helplessly in the taxi, completely locked down in traffic. He looked out the rear view window at the serpentine string of cars winding into the distance, and cursed whoever was assuredly holding up the entire city from the front of the line. The cab driver began to sing along to the radio, badly, in Spanish.

Irritated, Logan tapped on the divider. "Buddy, I'm paying you to get me to the airport on time. Do you understand? No karaoke, *airporte*."

Logan's phone rang. He pulled it from his pocket and answered. "Hola."

Never knowing which way the pendulum of Alexis' temperament would swing on any given day, Logan had grown to not expect any consistency of mood from her whatsoever. There were days when she showed up to work perky, polished and pleasant, ready to do the job and contribute to the environment. Those days were foretold by the appearance of a pair of breakneck stilettos and a pile of hair tucked up high into a professional wad. Between the shoes and the updo, she was always taller on the good days. Some days she was all lady and others she was an unmanageable gypsy. It was the mornings when she showed up to work in a sweater that hung off one shoulder and a hat of any kind that everyone steered clear and let her do whatever she wanted. Tomboy Lexy might as well have been El Nino, and not even Strauss had the guts to mess with her.

"*Hola, Senior,*" Alexis answered coolly. "I didn't realize *Virginia* was across the border." Her Spanish pronunciation of 'Virginia' sounded like Zorro himself.

"Feels like I could have been to Mexico and back already. I haven't even made it to the airport. Traffic is ridiculous."

"Well this should make you feel a little bit better. I just sent you the files."

"What files?"

"Guess what I saw this morning when I came in? Garrett and Cole swarming over your desk like a couple of vermin over fresh scraps... Which can mean only one thing: you left all your notes out for everyone to see."

"Oh my gosh. Tell me I didn't..."

"You did," she said, sounding bored.

"How much did they find?!" Logan shrieked.

"I don't know, but I managed to rescue most of your handwritten notes and to logout your computer."

"Most of them?"

"Not all of them, but enough for you to get started."

"It's bad enough that those two idiots are trying to sabotage me, but you too?"

"What's that supposed to mean?"

"I'm only a couple of steps ahead of those clowns as it is. Without all my research, I don't stand a chance!"

"I scanned as much at work as I could without getting caught. I'll send the rest tonight from home."

Logan mumbled something appreciative and hung up. Traffic still had not budged.

Virginia... why couldn't this guy have driven his truck off a bridge in Kentucky? Logan thought, peering sideways in his mind at the long journey ahead of him. His thoughts entangled the many questions he was pursuing for the rest of the excruciating time in the taxi.

When the cab finally arrived at the airport, Logan grabbed his luggage and threw the fare at the driver with no effort to be friendly. He rushed through the maze of security and eventually found the desk at his gate, and plopped his boarding pass down, panting.

"I'm supposed to be on this flight," he managed.

"I'm sorry sir, but the doors are now closed. We cannot allow anyone else on board."

Logan cracked his neck and gave the attendant a stinging glare. "What am I supposed to do now?" He bellowed, and turned to walk away.

"Sir," she called, "Let me see what I can do."

Logan stopped with his back to her and waited for a beat.

He could hear her nails clicking away on her keyboard. The level of frustration he was harboring was about to blow.

"Well, sir…" she waited for Logan to acknowledge her. He turned and set his bag on the floor. She smiled a plastic smile. "The next flight isn't until 2:30pm, but unfortunately it's full. The best I can do is put you on standby in case someone doesn't show up." She straightened and looked at Logan, waiting for his gleeful appreciation.

"Someone like me," he muttered, looking away. His sight rested on an ad for a rental car company. He cocked his head, considering the idea. "How far is the drive from Chicago to Virginia?"

She looked blank. "Virginia?"

He Googled it instead.

via I-65 S   10 h 7 min

613 miles

Ten minutes later, Logan walked through the sliding automatic glass doors with a giant rental company logo attached to a key and a wad of paperwork. He dumped his laptop bag, phone and jacket on the passenger seat of a shiny luxury-class sedan, programming Barwell, VA into the navigation system. He threw the car into reverse and didn't look back as he left the city shrinking in his rear view mirror.

*   *   *

Alexis sat erect in her chair, galaxies deep in internet research but not letting it affect her posture. A yellow legal pad was the only item on her desk other than the computer, the pen lodged in her hair and the perpetual mug of coffee never leaving her hand. There were no pictures or personal effects, no stacks of procrastination, no files or plants. Everything that crossed her desk was handled immediately and shifted to whoever needed it. After all, nothing was coming directly to her anyway; she was just an intern.

A list of leads that were still alive and connected in any way to the Capshaw case was growing on the legal pad. Alexis was not technically Logan's assistant, but having quickly learned that he was the only one in the building who could handle her, she had decided he was her only boss. Since she was lapping the productivity of every other intern in the office, Strauss let her do as she pleased. She knew she was on a need-to-know basis about everything, but the other girls in the office, being less domineering by far, kept her curiosity satiated about all things coming and going at the Chronicle. She, of course, then engineered the office chatter to her own liking and released it back into the grapevine.

Tracking down original witnesses from a crime that happened before she was born evoked a yawn and a stretch. After locking her notepad in the drawer and untangling her browser from the online web, she swung her skirted legs around and started toward the break room.

A. Rojas' cubicle was in the far corner opposite the elevators and the conference rooms. She liked surveying the sea of people whom she imagined herself to be smarter and shrewder than every morning as she walked her runway from one corner of the 18th floor to the other. She was the only intern with her own cubicle, confiscated from a staff member who had barely been released of his position before Alexis moved in and claimed his desk for herself. It was a bold move for sure, but it was nothing compared to her long-term goal of conquering the entire building and ruling it with an iron fist.

Reaching the lounge, the keen little Mexican girl in the high heels spotted the class clowns, Garrett and Cole. She rolled her heavily lashed brown eyes at the two of them as they approached.

"I see you are helping yourself to every food truck on Clark Street today," she chirped sweetly at Cole, who was chewing some kind of pressed sandwich wrapped in paper, grease pooling in the folds. He gave a good-natured salute with the meal in his hand, masticating ceaselessly.

"Your arteries are crying for mercy," Garrett added soberly, in a rare moment of agreement with Alexis. He was flipping through notes on a report, drinking a green smoothie. "You ought to be having one of these," he said with a slurp.

Alexis regarded them both with a carefully calculated expression of pity. "So tell me, Graves," she said, turning her back to them to brew herself the kind of rich, tacit coffee only stout homeland Mexican men could typically stand. "Has Strauss run your story about *Germs at the Gym* on the Health page yet?"

Garrett huffed. "No," he brooded. "Not yet." He'd only talked of nothing else for the last two weeks, the indignant truth of it all becoming his most passionate discourse.

"But you're not working out in an established facility anymore, due to the dangers of cross contamination?"

"No, I am now in favor of more *natural* athletics, such as outdoor boot camps and long distance hiking or running." His ego plumed. "It's better than machines and trainers. If you really know what you're doing, you don't need anyone else to motivate you."

Alexis stirred the cream. "So instead of weights you intend to use... what? Logs? Tree trunks? Small vehicles eventually?"

Her mockery was lost on him, as the only thing he cared about was being 'fit' and never wasted an opportunity to talk about any aspect of it. "Something like that. I prefer organic equipment, yes. My next column is going to be all about where in the city you can find natural resources for building muscle and trails for cardio. I even have a list of where to get free water all over Chicago."

"Mmm," Alexis said approvingly, mostly to the coffee. "And will there be accompanying recipes for making your own granola and plans to start an urban homestead?"

Cole laughed, and mystery sauce dripped onto his shirt. Garrett scowled. "No, *Alexis... that* would be on the *Home and Garden* page," he said, rolling his eyes at her inadequate knowledge of The Chronicle. "Besides, no one eats granola anymore."

"How obtuse of me," she smirked as she walked back past them with her steaming mug. "I'm sure Strauss will adore your ideas, Garrett, if he can rip his attention from your dramatically low readership." He frowned, realizing she'd been teasing him all along, which pleased Alexis. "Go on, hurry with the map of the water fountains, the population is waiting."

The two shook their heads at her, despising their own futile chances at a comeback.

"Your readers deserve to know which street corners they can drink tainted, diseased water from, and you are just the man to deliver that information. And Cole?" He looked up, knowing he was about to be accosted. "You chew like a llama."

CHAPTER FOUR

*L*ogan drove and drove, all day. He put the windows down, blared the music, and tried to clear out the rushing thoughts of his parents with the rushing wind and the miles rushing past.

He hardly noticed Indiana or Ohio, and finally started paying attention somewhere in West Virginia. It was there that he saw his first live cow. He slowed down and grinned like an idiot as he passed real livestock in a field, regarding him with wild eyes and lazy tails. He had never thought very hard about what the cheeseburger was like before it landed itself on a bun.

He saw signs for towns such as Everona, Oventop Springs, and Twin Farms. The last sixty miles were along a two-lane state route that twisted and turned into the horizon. The sun was setting from behind, making the landscape glow like a scene from a Thomas Kinkade print. Coasting and roaring down the road and keeping both hands on the wheel to handle the curves, Logan observed farmhouses set back from the road with large bronze stars hanging on their porches and barns. Sometimes he saw a mailbox out by the road with no house at all in sight. Living in the city his whole life, he was soothed by the low key vibes of the country and found himself wondering what life would be like in a place like this.

Contrary to the increasingly variant grade of the landscape, Logan felt himself leveling out. His head was clearing, and his focus was sharpening again. He was ready for whatever he found in this small town with old secrets.

The bucolic charm began to fade as the remaining mileage decreased. Run down trailer parks and an abandoned fair-grounds were the only scenery here. The closer Logan got, the more he felt that this was the kind of place to be if one wanted to get away with something.

Late in the evening, the car turned at a corner that was the home of the Mineral Park Pallet Company, and the halogen head lights cut through the dark rural stretch of highway. He took a long drag of coffee and slapped himself to reinvigorate his waning attention.

"Stay awake, Anders. You're almost there," He promised himself. He bested his previous volume and pushed the speakers to their limits, shoving down on the gas peddle.

Soon, a sign appeared that gave Logan his second wind.

WELCOME TO

BARWELL, VA

As the car veered anxiously around the last bend, a two story building painted a worn robins-egg-blue became visible through the trees. As Logan approached, his enthusiasm turned to doubt as he got closer to the Barwell Inn, the only hotel near the location of the old crime scene. The inn was small and dank, with cold windows lining both floors that looked out at the highway. A lone streetlamp burned putrid yellow light over the reservation office, a small addition to the right of the long bay of lodging rooms that looked like it had been constructed as an afterthought. Logan looked disbelievingly around. There was no way he would have willfully chosen to stay here, except that it was his only option, and the pictures online weren't accurate whatsoever.

He pulled into one of the many open parking spaces, wearily stepped onto the stoop covered in astro-turf and entered the drab office. All of the inner walls were constructed entirely from fake wood paneling, even the desk. There was nothing on the walls except a rack of brochures, a miner's peg-board with rows and rows of silver disks that hung behind the counter, and an analog clock that told Logan it was fifteen minutes after ten. An overly enthusiastic custodian came whistling from around the corner.

"Hello!" The clerk chimed. "Welcome to Barwell Inn & Suites. How can I help you tonight?" The twenty-something man with the poorly groomed facial hair appeared to think he owned this fine establishment but appeared also to be the type of guy who would live in his mother's basement. His name tag read 'Daniel Burns' in brass.

"I have a reservation under the name 'Anders'," Logan said vacantly.

Daniel looked at him, and his smile became tight and forced. He stared for a moment, and then suddenly whipped around and retrieved an outdated reservation book. "Alrighty, let me see here," he muttered, flipping through the thick, dusty pages. "Anders... let's see... Allen, no..."

He flipped back a few more pages. Logan looked around at the dingy interior. Dogeared business cards sat dormant in a card holder.

"Arthur... nope too far..."

Musty water pitchers and ceramic mugs lay stacked on a tray in the corner next to a gurgling coffee pot rattling its discontent, and a creepy cuckoo clock chirped the seconds away on the wall. The floors of this country gem were of the very lowest grade of vinyl, harboring many decades of stains and scuffs. In stark contrast, a sparkling new vending machine was keeping watch over the more inferior furnishings present in the lobby and brought into focus even more its forlorn surroundings.

"Anders with an 'N' right?" Daniel said, flipping a few pages the other way.

Logan rolled his eyes. *Unbelievable.* "Yep."

Daniel's finger nail ran down the page, scraping the linen sheet and irritating the life out of Logan. "Anders. Anders. Anders. There you are. Helps to be on the right page, doesn't it."

Logan smiled because that's what nice people do.

Daniel looked up and smiled back. "Have you ever stayed with us before?"

"First time," he managed.

"Well," Daniel replied, "You are in for a treat." He slammed the book shut. "All of our rooms come with two plush twin beds, access to unlimited cable television plus HBO on the weekends, your own thermostat so you can set the temperature exactly how you like it. What else... there's a vending machine by the stairs on both floors, but the ice machine is broken on your floor. Oh yeah, the in ground swimming pool... you won't find another one like it for fifty miles. Definitely going to want to try that out... well worth it. If you need extra towels just stop by the desk and I'll hook you up."

Logan was close to snapping Daniel's neck. "All I need right now is sleep, so could we speed this up?"

"Of course. Let me get you to sign in and I'll give you your key." Logan scribbled his name on the ancient log book and spun it back to him. He watched the proprietor take a key – not a key card, a very basic metal key - from a peg board hanging behind the desk. "Take the stairs at the end of the hall. Your room is the third door on the left." He was still smiling.

Logan nodded and walked toward the hallway.

"Mr. Anders?"

He stopped and turned around again. "Yes?"

"How long will you be staying with us?"

"I don't know."

Logan made his way down the musty hallway, feeling as though he was being watched. He found the firmly affixed room numbers 303, so secure because they were stickers. He turned the lock and entered a room with two twin beds, and fell face down on the loudly patterned comforter. In less exhausting circumstances, that would have been a very poor choice, but sleep was beckoning more insistently than the jangle of the AC unit, the blaring HBO special from room 305 and the rattling jake brakes from the semi trucks passing by outside. He eventually rolled over and saw his phone blinking with messages. Flipping through notifications, he realized his phone had been on vibrate all day, and he had never noticed.

"Call Sadie" He commanded Siri.

Back in their cramped apartment in Chicago, Sadie was grasping a pregnancy health magazine, trying to read but seeing nothing on the page for her incessant worrying about Logan. Her belly thundered in pain just as her cell phone rang. "Hey," she answered. Her teeth were chattering, and she sounded like she had been crying.

"Hey," Logan responded, offering no notice of the

chattering and the crying and the missed calls.

"How was your flight?" her voice was flat.

"Long story, but I made it."

"Story of my life."

"What's that supposed to mean?" He was way too tired to deal with criticism.

"Why does everything have to be a secret with you? Isn't that what married people are supposed to avoid? Dishonesty?" she unfurled her questions with pent up energy.

Logan was not ready for this conversation. "What do you want me to say?"

"How about that when you woke up this morning, you were actually thinking about me? That leaving me was the hardest decision that you ever made.... But you can't say that, can you? Because you didn't ask yourself how this would make me feel? Not even once... I love you, Logan Anders, but I need you to love me back."

Logan was silent. He had no response. They sat there, clutching their phones, hopelessly separated. Logan, unable to manage the pressure, mumbled a goodbye and hung up.

Sadie looked out the window at the park below and leaned her head on the glass. The autumn leaves shimmered as they rustled in the wind outside. There was something hopeless about the fall foliage, she thought. No matter how hard it holds on or how beautiful it makes itself to the world, it will eventually be overcome and fall silently, unheard, to the ground. There's no use trying to save something that can't survive. She closed her eyes as hot tears spilled over her cheeks and down the window pane, like drops of rain indoors.

KNOCK KNOCK KNOCK.

No… No, no I am asleep. Go away, Logan thought, clutching the bed as if protecting it from invaders.

BAM BAM BAM.

Good God you've got to be kidding me.

"Mr. Anders? Mr. Anders, are you awake?"

Daniel. It's Daniel. No use ignoring him, he won't go away.

Logan rolled out of bed and wobbled the door open, his eyes still closed.

"Oh good, you're up," Daniel said obliviously.

"Yep."

"Each morning, I hand deliver a *complimentary* newspaper to each and every room." He tipped the paper into Logan's hand and bowed slightly; the eccentric awkwardness was really getting old.

"Thanks, Daniel," Logan yawned, scratching his bed hair.

"What time is it?"

"Ten 'til seven," He answered brightly.

"Ah, thanks. And the Barwell Times couldn't wait until, say closer to ten 'til noon?" Logan glared through one open eyelid.

"The news waits for no man!" The innkeeper proclaimed. "You of all people should know that." And he continued down the hall.

Logan stood there, trying to process what Daniel was squawking about that early in the morning, and after a moment of empty observation, leaned out the doorway and shamelessly gawked as his host approached the next room.

BAM BAM BAM. "Mr. Long! I have your paper!" Daniel declared, seeming to not know how thin the walls were. An elderly man opened the door and accepted the paper with a scowl, and Daniel bowed in his singular way before passing on to the next guest in the corridor.

Logan eased his way back inside his room and closed the door, shaking his head. He tossed the paper on the side table and walked over to the coat closet, rumpling the curtain out of the way. It was empty. He opened the dresser drawers, but they were empty too.

"Where's my bag?" he asked the pathetic hotel room. He flopped down on the bed and mentally walked himself through the previous day, trying to remember, unawake, what he had done with the luggage. He finally concluded that he must have left it at the airport since he couldn't recall actually placing it in the rental car.

Sighing helplessly, he sat up and reopened the side table drawer, pulling out a Gideon Bible. Underneath was the local directory, with a huge picture of Daniel and a woman who appeared to be his mother plastered across the front. *Just when you think you've seen it all...*

He gave up on finding a decent listing and decided to clean up and try and find his way around this crazy town on his own. *How hard could it be to navigate Mayberry after all?* He wondered, shuddering at the hideous faces on the phone book.

After briskly freshening up, Logan made his way down the hallway. Daniel's back was to him, as he straightened brochures on a rack and whistled like a songbird. Logan slipped out the door unnoticed... so he thought.

"Mr. Anders! Where are you off to in such a hurry?" This guy had eyes in the back of his head.

"I'm desperate for a cup of coffee," Logan answered, defeated. "And some fresh air."

Daniel scurried to take this as a cue to pour a gelatinous substance into an ugly mug with the hotels logo in gold leaf and offer it to his guest with a flourish. "We have the best coffee in town. I'da brought you a cup earlier if I'd known."

Repulsed, Logan politely replied, "I appreciate that, but I have got to stretch my legs. Feels like I was driving for days."

Daniel shrugged his shoulders and took a thick slurp of the coffee-like sludge. "The Silver Diner is right next door. Not much of a walk but they have food if you're hungry. And fancy coffee for city folks." He grinned a simultaneously condescending, unaware, and decayed smile.

Logan shuddered and turned to leave, calling his thanks over his shoulder and pushing open the door.

"Mr. Anders…"

The escape plan was foiled again. "Yeah?"

"Tell Ole Missy I sent ya. If you show her your key, she'll charge it to your room."

Still looking away, his exit so close, Logan rolled his eyes and held up the key so it dangled from his forefinger. "Got it." He left before he could be stopped again.

Daniel watched Logan walk across the parking lot. He dialed a number on the rotary phone. *Ring, ring.* A female voice picked up. Daniel cupped his hand over the phone and muttered, "He's on the move."

CHAPTER FIVE

*L*ogan walked around the building to the Silver Diner, which was reflecting the early morning sunlight with a warm glow. It was a stereotypical 50's diner, lined with booths and a long bar. Logan walked in and was pleasantly surprised by its classic charm, and saw a young blonde girl serving plates to some elderly people at the bar. She was attractive and smiling, but there was no one else working out front so he figured she must be "Ole Missy." She looked up at him and told him to sit wherever he liked, and she'd be right with him.

Logan slid into a corner booth and looked around for a menu. He spotted one neatly tucked behind the napkin holder at the next booth and reached across to grab it just as the waitress approached.

"Sorry 'bout that," she frowned. "Easy to miss things when you're the only one workin' seven days a week." Logan smiled and waved his hand dismissively. She smacked her gum. "What can I get started for ya?" she asked, fussing with her ponytail and cocking her hips to one side.

Logan scanned the menu in vain for a meal that wasn't fried. "Do you have anything fresh?" He asked doubtfully.

"Um, we have fresh biscuits, fresh grits, fresh eggs, the fruit salad is canned though…and the hashbrowns are frozen if you wanna know the truth…"

Logan looked back down at the menu. "Breakfast of champions," he muttered.

"Hmm?" she asked brightly, leaning closer.

"Nothing." He snapped the menu closed. "Just coffee I guess. Black, please."

Missy reached for his menu. "You sure? We're known all over Carrollton County for our biscuits and gravy."

"Uh, coffee's fine, thanks."

"Alright. Your loss," she drawled and winked at him before retreating to the kitchen.

Logan cleared the flatware and placed it by the condiments before pulling out his cell phone and going through his morning routine of checking emails, texts, tweets, and sports scores. His email app had 15 notifications. Logan scrolled through them, all from Alexis. They were all scans of his notes.

Missy returned with a steaming pot of coffee and a beige mug, rimmed with a mustard yellow color. "I know you said you wanted it black, but I brought you some cream and sugar anyways." Logan was in the research coma and didn't even notice. "Hello… sir?" She touched his shoulder, but startled him so bad he swatted at her like a fly, bumping the full mug and dribbling coffee onto the table. "Oh! Sorry!" she giggled, covering her mouth. It was too late. She laughed out loud, and he laughed too, at himself. "You really get into that thing don't ya?" She chuckled, wiping the spilled coffee with her towel.

"Uh, yeah I guess so," Logan said, defenseless. "Sorry." Missy topped off his cup, and Logan stood up, extending his hand to her. "Logan Anders," he offered.

"I know who you are," she replied vaguely, shaking his hand anyway.

"Um, how is that? I've never been here before in my life." Paranoia crept into Logan's consciousness.

"Daniel's my cousin."

"Ah. Of course he is." Somehow that was a relief. He motioned for her to sit opposite him in the booth.

Missy sat happily, hunching over the table with terrible posture. "Let me guess, you're not from around here."

"I'm an investigative reporter with the Chicago Chronicle. It's a newspaper."

Missy sighed and looked bored. "So it's safe to assume you're here to solve the famous Capshaw family mystery?"

"It's never safe to assume anything. But yes, that's why I'm here."

Missy sat up. "Then you're a fool," she said abruptly.

Logan's eyebrows crept north. "Excuse me?"

"I've lived here my entire life," Missy whispered disdainfully. "Seen lots of reporters come and go. And they all leave the same, worse off than when they got here." She plunked her elbows onto the table for dramatic effect.

"What is that supposed to mean?" he asked coldly.

Missy leaned in closer. Logan did the same.

"Every year a handful of reporters roll into town," she mumbled. "Most not worth mentioning... but there was this one fella a couple years back. Claimed he'd finally gotten to the bottom of it all. He was obnoxious. Talked to everyone he saw. Left no stone unturned. He ended up making a lot of people mad."

"So what happened to him?" Logan asked in a hushed tone.

"Last time I saw him, he was sitting right where you're sitting. Scared out of his mind. He kept saying not to let the dead girl take him." Missy didn't bat an eye.

"What dead girl?"

"That night he dove out his hotel window... Into the empty pool." Missy sat back and folded her hands, expressionless.

Logan was irritated now. He leaned toward her closer,

squinting to confirm the name on her name tag. "Missy, is it? Thank you for sharing that *fascinating* story, but as I said, I am a *real* reporter. I don't work for a tabloid, and I don't believe in voodoo or the Boogie Man. And I certainly don't believe a ghost killed that guy. In fact, I doubt he even existed." He reclined also, matching her stance and letting his confidence ring through the stale air for a moment.

The waitress turned and stared out the window, shaking her head. "All you reporters are all the same. Stupid and reckless." She looked at Logan and slid out of the booth. "You go right ahead, dig too deep. But don't blame me when you can't get yourself out of the pit you've dug." With that, she flung her stained towel over her shoulder and began to walk away. Logan jumped up, determined not to leave empty-handed.

"What are you so afraid of?" he growled in a low voice.

"I'm afraid your time is up," Missy breathed, impatient.

Logan followed her to the kitchen door. "At least tell me where I can find the bridge," he insisted. "It's not on the map."

Missy turned before entering the kitchen and scanned the room. She studied him, eye to eye for a moment. Then she pulled out her pen and muttered, "And you call yourself a reporter." Logan ignored her and handed her a ticket book that was lying on the bar. She ripped off a sheet and sketched out a map on the back. Almost silently, she explained her drawing. "Follow Route 31 to the end of town. When you see Mitchel's Fillin' Station on the left, take the next right. The bridge is about a mile and a half down."

Logan grabbed for the ticket, but she held it firm and made him look at her. She stared him right in the eyes. "If anyone asks, you didn't get this from me. Okay?"

Logan met her gaze without a flinch. "Agreed."

She released the map, but the tension was thick. She smiled and pointed at his coffee. "You know, you didn't touch your joe."

Logan chortled at her petty attempt at lightening the mood. "I didn't come for the coffee," he said.

"Let me get you one to go," she insisted, her blonde ponytail bouncing after her. She poured a fresh serving into a styrofoam cup and snapped on the lid. "Be careful," she admonished, handing it to him. "Wouldn't want you to get burned."

Her deadpan warning was not lost on Logan. "I'll do my best," he assured, pulling out his room key. "Daniel said you could charge it to my room."

Missy began making a note of his room number, then closed the ledger. "It's on me. Least I can do for giving you a hard time and calling you names." She smiled.

Fickle, these folks.

"You think an 89 cent cup of coffee makes us even?" Logan chided back, a smile breaking his poker face. "Not even close."

"Well, come back later and I'll make it two."

Logan turned to leave. "I'll hold you to that."

He walked out, and Missy watched him through the glass door getting into his car and pulling out of the parking lot. She watched for a long time after he was gone. Finally, a chill scampered up her spine, and she went back to work.

Logan's rental car breezed down the two-lane street that ran through the heart of downtown. His vehicle screamed outsider, mostly because it was clean and new. Several antique shops, a beauty salon, laundry mat, liquor store... the backdrop through town was not impressive but was much friendlier in the daylight. Logan pulled out his phone and told Siri to call Alexis.

Ring, ring...

"Hello."

"Alexis, I need a favor."

"'Hi Alexis,'" She retorted, "'How are you? I'm good Logan, thanks for asking... thanks so much for spending your evening scanning files for me Alexis, you're the best...' that's the way normal people start a conversation before asking for a favor..."

"Alright, alright. You are the best. You satisfied?"

"Yes," she sighed. "That's all I've ever wanted."

"I need you to call the taxi place and the airport and find my luggage."

"Fine. Which shuttle service did you use?"

"American or United?" Logan guessed. "I don't remember. Just call them both."

"Do you know how many shuttle services there are at O'Hare?" Alexis whined. "This is going to take forever... and even if by some miracle I can find the right one, they probably won't talk to me because of Homeland Security. This is ridiculous."

"Lex, just figure it out and call me when you can tell me something I don't already know."

"How bout this? I do not work for you! You obviously haven't figured that one out yet."

"Very funny."

"Fine... I'll call the stupid airlines, but you owe me... big time."

"Thanks, Alexis," Logan grimaced sarcastically. "You're the best." He hung up just in time to see the gas station coming up on the left. Mitchel's Fillin' Station was definitely not a chain store. The entire station was brown – buildings, pumps, metal awning, even the trash barrels. But they were not painted brown. They were once white as snow, but now the rust stains had tainted every inch of the property. Even the water in the potholes in the parking lot were muddy brown. He eased off the road across the street from the rickety station and took his phone out, opening his email and scrolling through messages from Alexis.

"These better be in the right order," He muttered. He opened the email with the subject line 'SCAN #4' and read it aloud. "Mitchel's Fillin' Station. Ron Mitchel had testified to seeing Thomas Capshaw outside of his station at 1:29 am – the night of the accident. No other witnesses." Logan looked up at the dump. "Why was he all the way out here at one in the morning?" He wondered.

He slowly exited the car and walked across the street. There was no need to look both ways - there was not another soul in sight in either direction. Between dodging potholes in the 'parking lot', he scanned for clues but nothing seemed to be out of place. That was noteworthy in and of itself.

A lifted pickup truck pulled into the only working pump on the left side of the building. A burly man well over six feet tall squeezed out and swung the gas nozzle out of the cradle. Logan could hear the pump whirring. The man ignored Logan, patiently pumped his gas, and replaced the nozzle. His truck had no gas cap or fuel door for that matter to worry about.

"How you doing?" Logan called.

"Just fine," The man answered. Not very conversational.

"Mind if I ask you a couple of questions?" Logan asked

energetically.

"Depends on the questions and who's ask'n."

"My name is Logan Anders; I'm a reporter for the Chicago Chronicle." He let his introduction rest in the air.

Out of nowhere the burly man yelled in the direction of the shop. "Hey Mitch!" he called. He looked at Logan for the first time, with churlish eyes and thin lips.

A thick, bearded man who must be Mitch came out of the not-so-convenient store carrying a shotgun. The burly man yelled to him, "I thought you said you got rid of all the rats?"

"So did I," the proprietor threatened.

"...Says he's a reporter from Chicago," the burly man said, nodding at Logan.

Without blinking an eye, Mitch pumped a shell into the chamber and aimed it straight at the trespassing reporter. "I dunno how 'ey do things up north," he said menacingly to Logan, "but 'round here, soliciting is a punishable offense." He articulated cautiously so he would not be misunderstood.

Logan shot his hands up like the tiny flags kids wave at a Memorial Day parade. "Whoa," he said, "Ok now. This is just a big misunderstanding."

Mitch sneered. "I understand that you walked onto my property – stuck your nose where it don't belong and now you're tellin' me I don't know what I'm talkin' about."

"No sir," Logan stuttered. "I mean, I can see how what I did could make you feel that way... So I'm going to take a step back now." Logan backed away and the gun was lowered. Logan felt blood drain from his face and then rush back to it, hot. Amidst the unexpected confrontation, Logan noted that the business hours on the door listed closing time at 9 pm. He looked back at the redneck with the gun. "I was 100% wrong... I apologize for that, sir."

Mitch backed toward the door. "I forgive you. Now you have 'till the count o' three to get off my property."

Logan scrambled for his car. A warning shot went off into the sky from Mitch's gun, making Logan jump, and fumble starting the car. He started the engine with trembling hands and peppered the guardrail with dirt as he peeled onto the asphalt road. He sped off, veering right around a bent up stop sign and heading out of sight down a side street with an unpainted sign. Breathing husky breaths of panic, he wound through the trees like a snake in tall grass. The one and a half lane road was covered with a canopy of foliage, and rays of sunlight cut through the low-lying fog like lasers.

Logan replayed the bizarre encounter he had just had, trying to manhandle this interaction into having some productive purpose. He immediately wondered why he was all the way out here trying to act like a private detective instead of a proper reporter who knocks on doors and records perfunctory interview facts. Checking himself in the rear view mirror and seeing the color had returned to his face, he took a deep breath and sped up a little, back on task. After that confrontation, he was more determined than ever to solve this case. He avoided the rear view mirror; he wasn't looking back. But soon he came up fast to a yellow sign screaming SLOW 15... a near 90-degree hairpin turn was less than 200 feet away. He slammed on the brakes and nearly ran into the ditch, but managed to keep the car on course.

Pine needles and dust covered the once clean car. First having a gun shoved in his face and now almost running off the road... Logan's nerves were crackling. He pulled off the road and checked for any damage. As he circled the front fender, he saw what was beyond the curve that almost just killed him. The mountain forest cleared to reveal a bridge.

CHAPTER SIX

A quiet reverence settled over him. He allowed it to sink in that an entire family may have been killed here. Slowly and deliberately he walked down the center of the road until he reached the edge of the drop-off, where there was a tiny sign that labeled this as the Carrollton Bridge. "No wonder it wasn't on the map," Logan hissed. What was locally known as the Miners Gap Bridge stretched for a half mile in front of him, a narrow single lane construction made entirely of steel. Far below, guarded on the western side by a solid slope of rocks, was the rushing Carrollton River.

Diagonal braces secured the road to the mountains on either side and as he walked out to the middle of the bridge, Logan counted each of its triangular trusses. When he got to number thirty-seven he decided he was halfway across, and stopped to study the water churning beneath his feet and an empty sky stretched out above him. Rotating a full circle, he searched for a sense of truth about what actually happened there, listening for the forests to whisper to him what they had seen.

He looked around for some time but learned nothing. Walking back towards his car, he noticed two sets of concrete pillars that protected the only possible way down to the water. Thick cables strung each pillar to the next and beyond the pillars was a chain link fence, about six feet tall.

Curious.

Pulling the cell phone from his pocket, Logan opened his email again and pulled up scan #3. Scrolling to a black and white photo of the bridge from the night of the accident, he held the phone out in front of him, comparing his position to the photo. He walked around until they both matched.

"What's the difference?" He asked himself.

He studied the photo for several minutes, waiting for a revelation.

"How could a truck accidentally go off this bridge? Doesn't make sense."

The photo and the present location matched exactly. Unsatisfied, Logan walked back onto the bridge and examined the concrete barriers and fencing from the opposite direction. Nothing stood out... again. This was more than a feeling or wishful thinking to him. Like an ancient wind blowing in his soul, this was a guttural instinct. He scrutinized the photo, then the scene, over and over, patiently asking questions into the thin mountain air to somehow draw out its secrets and make the past come into focus.

"They had to have missed something," He assured himself. "It was 1988, after all." And then, click. Realization.

Back in the rental car, Logan spun back toward town, the bridge disappearing in the rear view mirror. The forest was blurring by. His cell phone was mounted to the dash and on speaker, and Alexis was sounding annoyed.

"It's only been twenty minutes and no I haven't called the airport..."

"You can do that later," Logan interrupted. "I have something more important for you to do." He noticed the untouched cup of coffee from the Silver Diner in the cup holder.

"Oh goody," Alexis chortled. Although Logan was the only one she would allow to tell her what to do, she still disliked it.

Logan pulled the lid off the cup with his teeth, the coffee still impressively warm. "I just came from the scene of the crime."

"So you're convinced they were murdered?" Alexis perked up.

Logan sipped the coffee but burnt his lips, sputtering. "Oh man that's still hot... No, but I am convinced that at least one crime or maybe several crimes have been committed. I'm heading to the courthouse right now to take a look at the original police reports. I have a sneaky suspicion that they have been altered."

"Why's that?"

"The photos of the bridge that I downloaded from the courthouse website were supposedly from two and a half decades ago, but they matched perfectly with the present location."

"Interesting. So what do you want me to do?" Alexis was suddenly cooperative.

"If I can't trust the police reports, I'll need to reinterview the witnesses to find out the truth for myself."

"There was only one, remember?"

"Lex, there was only one in the official report. Do you really think no one else was around or knew what was happening? It will just take some digging."

Alexis didn't respond right away. "You know it's haunted down there," she said cautiously.

Logan blew steam from his coffee.

Alexis sighed. "I'll see what I can do," she promised.

Alexis slipped the phone into its cradle and bolted from her chair in the direction of the elevator. She checked her watch: 9:18 AM, Central Standard Time. She could be down to the basement and back before her 10 o'clock coffee break.

Nervously, she drummed her fingers on her folded arms as

the elevator descended. "If a truck goes off a bridge in the middle of the night, and no one is around to hear it, does it still make a sound?" She grinned at her own mastery of American English humor. Then the doors opened, and her smile tightened as her gaze wandered from the long hallway in front of her, and she looked up at the ceiling as her heels clicked their rhythm on the ancient floor. "If a truck with three people goes off a bridge in the middle of the night... why isn't there anyone around to hear it anyway... how did it go over? Did someone force them off the bridge or did they kill themselves? Why would they do that? Or why would someone else do that to them? Foul-play maybe." She shuddered. "Or maybe... *fantasma*..." She reached the very deepest bowels of the Chicago Chronicle building and heaved the swinging door open.

Everyone at the Chronicle knew there was a ghost in the basement, but it was also good luck if you could find the courage to face him. The stories over the years had grown and evolved and were now legends of a spirit who was perhaps not sinister, but had a devious sense of humor. Rumor had it that the last of the typesetters, Charlie Gloss, had been killed when one of the monstrous, art deco printing presses jangled itself loose from its constructs and flung a mechanical arm right into Charlie's jugular. The whole tragic thing had been sadly written off as a workplace disaster, and new equipment had been brought in, and the news kept coming. Some of the papers that day had been sprayed with blood, but the newsies delivered them anyway. Bloody newspapers are always sensational.

It wasn't until some time later when someone found

Charlie's familiar gray golf hat down in the basement, at the end of the long hall, up high on top of a shelf, with Charlie's blood across one side, that the whispers of his or someone's ghost ruminated among the staff. Charlie always wore his hat; no one had ever seen him without it, but no one could remember for certain whether or not it had been on his head the day he died. He had in fact been buried without it. When strange and mischievous things started happening at the Chronicle shortly after his wake, that exacerbated the rumors and gave everyone something new to gossip about around the coffee machines.

The basement was now littered with old pieces of printing equipment, scattered and forgotten like a graveyard of stories that are no longer relevant, just like the machines that proclaimed them. Thousands of stories that made Chicagoans clutch their chests in fear or look wide-eyed at their spouses were just phantom memories now. The next acts of terrific human error marched along through the newspapers in ghastly procession. People eventually either tired of the static of crime and impending doom or they just stopped buying the paper, and nowadays the neat bundle of news that sat on the doorsteps of America had been overshadowed by the instant gratification of technology. Truthfully, whether there really was a ghost or not, the modern industry for printed news was slowing down, and could be coming close to as unceremonious of a death as poor old Charlie Gloss.

Alexis pushed herself to walk boldly through the dimly lit aisles, along the uninteresting towers of boxes and files and backlogs. She invisibly trembled like a freshly bathed

Chihuahua. Spirits and ghosts are something Mexicans take seriously. Finally, she reached the back wall and its long bay of file cabinets. She looked at the whole footprint of the twenty-one stories that rose nobly above the street, marveling for a moment at the vast nature of this building and its lifespan. They never include the basement in the number of floors there are in a building like this, maybe so that unspeakable things can happen off the grid. She shook her head and tried to get her mind on the task at hand. Locating the "C" drawer, she picked through the dog-eared and dusty folders until her smooth, small hand found the label that simply said, 'Capshaw.' She held her breath as she pulled it out from the sheaths of other files. "Wow. I found something," she murmured.

The file drawer slammed shut, but it was the sight of Garrett Graves leaning against the wall on the other side that made Alexis jump. "What are you doing down here?" she jeered, trying to breathe normally.

Garrett chuckled. "Whatsamatter chica? Did I startle you?"

Alexis squeezed her eyes shut and bit her tongue. She hated being called *chica*. Garrett was a perpetual waste of time, and to a Latina with something to prove in an office full of men, a loitering ivy-leaguer couldn't be more useless. She decided to let him live and looked up at him, Spanish fire on full display. "Your ego, it has grown since the last time I saw you. It terrified me," she replied, dripping with lava and sashaying past him with her nose in the air. He snickered with entertainment and followed.

"So how's Anders coming along with his wild goose

chase?" he inquired with a rigorous attempt at innocence.

"Oh, that? He caught the guy who did it yesterday," she sighed falsely.

Garrett's eyes popped open wide. Then a sly smile slipped across his lips. "Yeah I bet. There's no way. He hasn't been out there 48 hours yet." She ignored him, and it made him nervous. He made light of the whole thing all the way back up to the busy copy room. There, Alexis turned to him in the doorway, not allowing him to pass, and gave him a look that would scald the demons in hell.

"Logan is half way across the country digging up more ghosts and skeletons than you'll ever see in your life," she challenged, getting the attention of those nearby. "That's what a journalist does; they go after their story. And this story is skyscrapers above your head, Graves. Don't think I'm above yanking you back down to the basement by your crispy hair and showing you where you can shove your jokes. Logan Anders is ten times the reporter you'll ever be; you are nothing but a local dimwit paperboy."

He flushed with embarrassment, and Alexis wheeled around and pranced away. Everyone else went back to making copies.

Logan drained his cup, and his stomach lurched. *Terrible coffee*, he lamented. He parked and approached the courthouse past the billowing American flag and under towering white pillars. Inside, he was immediately greeted by a metal detector and two members of the sheriff's department. The more senior of the two was a hard as bricks officer who wore a name badge that identified him as Sheriff Crutcher. Logan was asked gruffly to raise his arms over his head like a railroad crossing guard. After being scanned, the shorter, more nervous deputy held out a plastic container in Logan's direction.

"Empty your pockets," he instructed in a voice like a church mouse. "Put any metal objects and electronic devices in the bucket."

Logan dropped his wallet, keys and cell phone into the container and started through the detector. On the other side, Sheriff Crutcher halted him with a thick hand.

"Hold up, son! You gotta wait till I wave you through… back up and let's do it again."

Logan hated being called 'son', but he understood how to respect authority. He complied by waiting for the Sheriff to wave him through, which he did without setting off the alarm. The stocky deputy handed him the container again, and Logan quickly shoved his items back into his pockets.

"Where's the fire, son?" the Sheriff asked suspiciously.

"The whole world's on fire. Sometimes you just can't see it," was Logan's dark response.

The sheriff scratched the back of his precise military haircut. Then he slipped his thumbs into his utility belt, resting his right hand comfortably on the handle of his pistol. He began to laugh, then looked over at his deputy.

"Now don't that beat all," he chuckled sarcastically. "You a poet or something, son?"

Ignoring the ridicule, Logan redirected the conversation. "Only on weekends. Who do I speak with about public records?"

The deputy piped up for the first time. "You'll want to talk to the clerks office." Logan noticed the sheriff shoot him a withering look, and he immediately clammed back up and turned his back, knowing his place.

"What are you hoping to find?" the sheriff asked, squinting his eyes.

Logan sized him up. "A little of this, a little of that…"

"I hope none of *this* or *that* took place before 2005… 'cause tragically, all our records before then were destroyed in a horrific fire." The Sheriff locked his jaw and looked satisfied with himself.

Logan didn't blink and stared for a moment. "You've got to be kidding."

"I wouldn't joke about something like 'at," Sheriff Crutcher replied with thinly veiled artificial sorrow.

"So you're telling me that every stitch of paper before seven years ago is gone."

"If it wasn't digitized… I'm afraid so."

"Was the D.A. killed in the fire also?"

The sheriff cocked his head and looked over at the deputy. "I think I'm gonna like havin' this one around." He turned back to Logan with a grin full of huge teeth. "Down the hall. Take a left then another left. She'll be on the right."

Logan turned on his heel. "Much obliged."

"Son…"

Logan halted and looked over his shoulder.

"Want me to send Smitty to assist you?" he nodded at the deputy. "Wouldn't want you to get lost along the way."

"I think I can manage," Logan said, turning back to the hallway. *This guy takes his job way too seriously*, he thought.

The sheriff motioned with a shift of his eyes for the deputy to follow Logan.

A silver-haired watchdog receptionist looked up as Logan entered the office and neared her massive barricade of a desk. Her gauzy white hair spread loosely over her shoulders, being propped back from her eyes with a dark headband. She peered at him curiously over her glasses with eyes so blue he could see them from across the room. J. HESS flickered from her brass name tag. She kept typing on her ancient typewriter and asked if he could be helped.

"Yes… I would like to speak with District Attorney Claridge."

"Do you have an appointment?" the gatekeeper asked, still typing.

"No ma'am, but..."

"Then it's impossible," she assured bluntly.

Logan gritted his teeth and took a shallow breath. "Ok, then I'd like to make an appointment."

"Can you come three weeks from Friday?"

"Three weeks!" Logan was stunned.

"That's the best I can do."

"I just need to ask a couple questions."

The receptionist stopped typing and made eye contact for the first time. "You already have."

Logan's blood boiled. "Could you notify me if anyone cancels in the next day or two?" he asked with forced civility, pounding a business card on the counter.

"That's highly unlikely," she replied, distracted, squinting her eyes to look at him.

Exasperated, Logan turned to leave. The elderly receptionist seemed to soften a bit. "You remind me of my nephew," she said, almost calling after him. "He would be about your age... if he were still alive."

Logan froze, sensing a small window of opportunity. He

turned and said, "Oh really? What was his name?"

Her eyes glassed over as she became lost in memories of the past. Logan pretended to admire a framed picture of a small white dog with a black head on the edge of the desk. After a few awkward moments, Logan turned to leave again.

"There may be another recourse," the receptionist blurted.

Logan turned again. She motioned him to come closer. He leaned on the counter, trying not to seem too eager. "Ms. Claridge is heading out of town tomorrow morning," she mumbled. "She's the featured speaker at a criminal justice seminar in Atlanta... almost always stops by here to make sure everything's in order before she leaves town. You might be able to catch her then."

"What time?" Logan asked.

"Between 8:30 and 9."

"Thank you very much," Logan sighed.

The receptionist turned and again began typing. "Don't be late," she called as Logan swung out the door.

"I never am," he called back.

The door closed with a thud, and Logan stood in the empty hallway. His stomach was feeling belligerent from the cheap coffee, and his head was starting to pound. He took a rattled breath, and since the corridor was empty of any other people, he dialed Alexis.

"Hey," he barked as soon as she answered. "I need you to get me any and all records, articles, a full history report on this Capshaw guy. Anyone he knew, anyone who knew him."

"Um, I'm working on it, but they are probably all *dead*," Alexis complained, not thrilled with the thought of all that research.

"If none of them are alive, then find the ones who are dead," Logan commanded. "We've got to crack something."

She sighed, and mocked him silently. "I'll send everything I can find," she promised. They both hung up.

He looked up and noticed a side hall shooting off the main walkway. The entrance had been covered with thick opaque plastic. He couldn't resist. Making sure the coast was clear, he ducked around the flimsy barrier.

"What do we have here..." he wondered to himself. The walls were covered in black soot. Exposed wires and insulation hung down through giant holes in the drop ceiling. Logan ignored his natural instincts to turn back and forged ahead.

At the far end of the hall stood a 1950's style door with a large frosted glass window and bold painted lettering.

RECORDS ROOM

Logan reached a hand for the knob and turned it slowly. Locked. *Of course you're locked*, he thought.

He reached into his back pocket and retrieved his wallet. Thumbing through his credit cards to find the most disposable one, he checked again to make sure the coast was clear before cramming it into the door jamb, working the lock. *Hurry up Anders, hurry up.*

CLICK CLOP CLICK CLOP. Someone was walking down the main hallway. Logan flushed and jiggled the door handle and credit card faster and faster, hearing the footsteps approach. *Let go… you stupid lock…*

POP. The lock sprung just in time for Logan to hop inside the door and gently push it shut. He breathed a flustered sigh of relief and listened for the footsteps to continue down the hallway before moving a muscle. He almost felt like vomiting.

The title "records room" had to be a joke, he concluded. This room looked more like a closet full of knick-knacks. Multiple sized and colored filing cabinets propped up one wall, and open faced shelving units held cardboard filing boxes on another wall. Even a few broken desks from the high school were haphazardly stored there. Logan fired up the flash light app on his phone. Dust particles lingered in the air as he pried open one of the tallest filing cabinets and sifted through the folders. He closed the drawer, unsatisfied. He opened another, and another, and repeated the cycle for several minutes. Nothing. The beam of his flashlight swept from box to box, from shelf to shelf. *There's got to be something here somewhere*, he thought. Frustrated, he put his hands behind his head and looked up at the ceiling, and noticed something slid all the way to the back of the top shelf.

Using the shelving unit as a ladder, he climbed up and retrieved a unique looking box. All the other filing boxes were modern and white. This one was black, sturdy, and well made – like they would have made filing boxes twenty-five years ago. He slid the lid off and revealed that it was not a file box at all, but an evidence box. "Now we're talking," Logan breathed.

Shards of glass from a windshield, paint samples scraped from rocks, photos of tire tracks, personal items from a home, handwritten witness testimonies... it was from the accident.

Logan was shaking with excitement, and his chest filled with his own surreptitious capability. As he leafed through the box, a rash of goose bumps went down his arms, and his mind started to race trying to figure out how to get this box out of the building. Then he felt his nose fill with something else entirely. He shoved himself off of the floor, which was filling with putrid fumes.

Flailing to back away he smacked his left hand hard on the metal shelf and stumbled backward into the desks, and his vision suddenly blurred. Like flash bulbs from the 1920's, explosions of light crackled all over the room. The loud noises shook him to his core as the room started spinning. Everywhere he turned, he became more clouded and confused, as if he were drowning with air in his lungs.

Logan rushed out of the room and toward the main hallway, knocking into people as he left the corridor. He fell into a plant and tripped someone, having no control over himself. He blindly made it to the lobby and tore through the front door, as Sheriff Crutcher watched, unmoving.

Logan stumbled feverishly toward the car, opening the door just as his strength gave out and he collapsed in slow motion to the ground.

CHAPTER SEVEN

"*R*ealmente?! This is what you bring me?" A deluge of unintelligible Spanish came forth, her disdain apparent although no one knew exactly what Alexis was saying. A slim list of leads were compiled on a single piece of paper, the efforts of Marcus and Samantha, two young, naïve interns who were now cowering in fear upon delivery of their inferior work. With a temper hotter than ghost peppers and the confidence of a well-heeled girl with curves, she was unmistakably convinced she was the ruler of all she surveyed. At the Chronicle, the staff of interns were all her *campesinos*. As her *R*'s trilled and her *J*'s hushed themselves, a tirade of Iberian disappointment descended on everyone within earshot. Those who could understand anything were ashamed to hear it, and the rest just shook their heads in disgrace knowing they must somehow be to blame.

Just as her hand made its way onto one hip and the other hand began wagging in the faces of the poor new kids, Steven Strauss walked by. Alexis slipped seamlessly into a tone of good humor and workplace fun and appeared to her boss to be telling jokes and boosting morale. She flashed him a winning smile and kept right on scolding her poor workmates with an expression like one who was sharing news of something silly her neighbor's baby had done the night before. The conflict of being poisonously reprimanded with a friendly grin in a language you don't understand was a thing of terror to endure, and the girl started to cry in bewilderment. A deadly glare was delivered, and she choked herself silent until Mr. Strauss was long down the hall. It gave Alexis a moment to collect herself.

"This is pathetic," she scolded with unnerving calm. "Anders is in the dusty backwoods of the *East*" - the disgust apparent in her voice – "and not one of us here in civilization is gonna rest until he has every resource in cyberspace. Unless you want to be shipped off to the mountains, tied to a wagon and have moonshine dumped down your throat, you'll get Logan the information he needs to bring back a story and impress Strauss." The two looked at each other in horror, wondering if wagons and moonshine were all there was in existence in dusty Virginia. Having never been to the East coast, they were inclined to believe her; regardless, if you'd lived your whole life in Virginia and knew there were no such threats, you'd think twice if Alexis Rojas told you that's what you'd get.

A dejected Marcus and a sniffling Samantha departed to hunt down intel on the Capshaw story at the crack of Alexis snapping her fingers. As they ran in opposite directions simply to distance themselves so they could think clearly, the self-elected queen drank her bitter coffee deeply and drained her cup in one consecutive swill. Crumpling the foam cup and tossing it in the garbage, she marched in triumph back down the bay of cubicles and back to her desk, where she applied a fresh coat of red lipstick and took out her frustrations vehemently on a rubber stress ball.

Drool dripped onto Logan's pillow. He was fully dressed and lying on top of the ugly floral comforter once more. The cell phone next to him started ringing, slowly drawing him into consciousness. He made no attempt to answer it, but groaned as he rolled over onto his back and tried to wake up. Once the room was silent again, Logan thought to himself, *What happened to me? Did someone try to poison me? Maybe I was drugged.* Then he opened his eyes and thought, How did I get back here? The cell phone rang again. Without looking, he fumbled for the talk button and said, "Hello?"

"Hello? Is that all you can say to me?" Sadie was frantic. "I've been worried sick. I thought something terrible had happened to you…"

"Sadie?" Logan blinked.

"I've been calling you all day. Why didn't you answer your phone?"

"What? What time is it?" He pulled the phone away from his face and struggled to read the time. It was nine o'clock at night.

"Logan, are you alright? You don't sound alright…

Logan?"

Logan stumbled to the window and ripped back the curtain. His car was parked in the same spot it had been this morning.

"Logan, you're scaring me," Sadie whimpered.

"I'm still here. I guess I just lost track of time."

The couple sat silently longing for each other. "I miss you," Sadie whispered, softening.

"I miss you too," Logan whispered back, sitting back down. He heard her voice catch on the other side of the line, and saw in his mind's eye a tear roll down her cheek.

"I don't know how to do this," she said. "You keep pushing me away and I don't know why."

Logan groaned. "Do we have to do this again tonight?"

"Yes we do," Sadie cried angrily. "Maybe it was too much to expect you to deal with everything the way I think I would... but we can't do this without each other... I can't do this without you."

Logan sat up on the bed. "I missed their anniversary dinner," he heard himself say, sounding like a little boy. "Now they are gone. I'll never see them again..."

"Solving this case will not bring them back, babe," Sadie said, gently but firmly.

"I'm not doing this for them," Logan said, without anger or impatience. "I'm doing this for us."

Sadie paused. "For us?! How on earth does this help us? Logan! Why don't you just come home?"

"I can't come home, not without a story."

"Why not?" Sadie asked suspiciously.

"I'll get fired, Sadie… I made a deal with Mr. Strauss that I'd come back with a story… or I wouldn't come back at all."

"So you lied to me," Sadie accused. "Why would you do that? We don't do that… at least I thought…"

"I was afraid of losing you! I can't lose anyone else."

"I didn't marry you for your job. I married you because I love you… and because I can't live without you… Please come home."

Logan was silent. He shook his head. "I'm sorry. I just can't."

He unceremoniously hung up and laid back on the bed for several moments, but couldn't relax. He walked back over to the window and pulled back the curtains. His gaze wandered to the pool, and he realized the pool was empty. Completely empty.

Logan shuddered and moved back to the bed, trying to come up with a new game plan. After a quick shower and redressing in his only present clothing, he worked on his laptop late into the night trying to dig up more dirt. He looked into the mayor, the sheriff and deputy, Missy, Daniel… everyone.

Hours later, Logan had fallen asleep again, sprawled out on top of the covers. He slept fitfully, being tormented in his dreams by an annoying small white dog with a black head.

Knock Knock Knock.

Logan's body shot off the pillow like someone being raised from the dead. He opened the door just wide enough to reach out and take the all-fired important newspaper and say, "Thanks." He retreated inside to the shelter of his room. "You're welcome," he heard Daniel say from the other side. Logan sighed with relief that he wasn't being annoyed to death. Not hearing anything, he stepped back over to the door and peered through the peep-hole. Daniel wasn't standing there. He flung open the door and looked both ways. No one was there!

Logan backed into the room and slammed the door shut. He reached for the deadbolt and chain, but they weren't there. Like a blind man, he felt up and down the door, not believing his eyes.

The doorknob, frame, and even the hinges were missing. He was trapped.

Claustrophobia was kicking in fast, and his throat was closing. He was like a chained tiger being taunted, struggling to escape the mounting terror. As he turned to reach for the bed, Daniel was standing right behind him.

"Mr. Anders," he leered. "Anders, is it…" The room started tilting and Daniel took a step toward him as Logan stumbled out from in front of the door. Daniel swung wide and missed, but Logan could smell his breath.

"Get away from me, you freak!" He screamed. He turned and ran toward the only apparent escape: the window. In a panic, he dove right through the glass and plummeted headfirst toward the empty pool. His eyes and mouth gaped wide as an ungodly scream erupted from deep inside him.

A pickup truck with its headlights off rolled into the parking lot of the Mineral Pallet Company and slowed to a stop. The engine kept running, but no one got out. Fully ten minutes later a dark green sedan crept up to the warehouse, also not using headlights, and pulled up beside the truck and stayed running.

A man opened the truck door and couldn't help his heavy boots from crunching the gravel as he started to walk around to the driver's side of the car. But right as he reached the bumpers, he saw lights coming down the long stretch of highway. He immediately leapt back into his truck and the car barely waited for him to move before peeling away and lurching onto the state route that left the highway at this particular junction. The truck pulled into the shadows of the lumber yard and waited for the vehicle to pass before backing out and heading the opposite direction, back towards town. His lights stayed off until he was over the hill.

*   *   *

The clock on the night stand read 8:55 AM.

Logan's eyes opened, and he found himself in the fetal position in the hotel bed, the covers pulled up over his head. His face popped out to see if the coast was clear. "No, no, no, no…" Logan moaned, seeing the time, as he fled from the bed. Like a bat out of hell, he tore out of the room, unconcerned about his appearance.

He pounded down the stairs and grabbed a handful of mints from the candy dish in the lobby on his way out the door. Jumping into his car, he slammed the door and punched the key into the ignition. The clock read 8:58. *Shoot!*

He sped across town; his mind racing with his many problems. He rubbed his eyes and chewed the mints with fury as he tried to collect himself and gird up for a possible confrontation with the D.A. He careened luckily into a parking space right outside the courthouse. He jumped out of the car and dashed up to the doors, slowing down at the metal detectors. He avoided making eye contact with the sheriff and deputy. They didn't get the hint.

"Had quite a spell here the other day, didn't you son?" The sheriff drawled.

Logan squared his shoulders and eyed him. "I'm fine. Except I'm about to be late for an important meeting. Can we hurry this up… please?"

After shuffling through security, Logan blazed to the

D.A.'s office. The blinds were drawn, and the door was locked. He shoved his hands into his pockets, perplexed. Then the elderly secretary wheeled a cart around the corner. Logan watched her walk toward him, unhurried, one caster squeaking. She finally stopped right next to him.

"I told you not to be late," she chided. Then she looked down the hallway and squeaked along. Logan watched until she disappeared around another corner. After a beat, a puzzled expression crossed his face. He looked around for the odd hallway that led to the records room. But now, it was nowhere in sight.

The wall opposite the D.A.'s office was completely solid now. No side hallway, no doors. He slid his palm across the surface, then gave the wall a couple of raps to make sure it wasn't just a façade. It was real alright.

Outside the courthouse, Logan trudged across the lawn and collapsed on a park bench. He suddenly pulled out his cell phone and pulled up his photo gallery. *Gone.* He opened his email app. *Gone.* His leg began fidgeting uncontrollably. His knuckles turned white, and his neck turned red as he fought to keep from erupting with anger and frustration.

He looked up at the parking lot, the mail truck on the corner, the shops along the side street. Was this real? He was losing his conviction that this was not all just a silly dream. Unexplainable things don't happen in real life. Logan was utterly at a loss for what to do next, since every step he took seemed to lead in a giant circle. He mentally counted off seven reasons why he should calmly get in his rental car, drive away, and return to the city from whence he came. A place where crime was normal and predictable, and there was a public servant on every block. The only reason to stay here was Steven Strauss. But there were other jobs out there, right?

"Get it together, Anders," he told himself. "There's a logical explanation for all of this... you saw what you saw... You're not crazy..."

"Of course you're crazy," A voice said from behind Logan. He froze. "Don't turn around," the voice said. *Oh good, it's not in my head*, Logan thought. "Only crazy people keep asking the same questions the same way and expect to get different answers."

Logan started to turn around slowly. "What?" he asked.

"I said don't turn around," the voice snapped. Logan halted and looked back to the parking lot in front of him. "You think that they are in on the cover-up – right?"

"Right," Logan nodded.

"But you keep knocking on the front door hoping they'll let you in. They won't," the voice assured.

Logan didn't recognize the voice, but it was a woman. "Then what am I supposed to do?" he pled.

"Find someone who hates this town more than you do," came the reply.

Logan couldn't stand it anymore and whipped around,

shouting, "Well, who?!"

There was no one there.

Daniel sat perched on a vinyl bar stool behind the motel's humble front desk reading the local paper, The Porch Dweller. The front door chimed. Daniel quickly stowed his paper and grinned widely, until he saw who had entered.

"Butch," he nodded without a shred of energy.

"Burns," the burly man nodded back, equally robotic. The two men locked eyes for a moment.

Daniel opened the paper back up and cleared his throat. "What can I do for you, Butch?" he muttered, scanning the sports section casually.

The bully slowly plunked across the room in his thick boots and manually lowered the newspaper from Daniel's nose. Daniel glanced up but settled his concentration on the man's top button. "I want to know where that nosy reporter is staying," Butch challenged.

"HIPPA says I can't tell you that," Daniel assured with false bravado.

"My gun says you *can* tell me that," Butch threatened.

Six beads of sweat formed immediately on the back of Daniel's neck. He swallowed and looked up at Butch. "I don't think the D.A. would allow that," he advised quietly.

The insolent man took a pencil from the counter and snapped it in half, and muttered something hideous in Daniel's face before swaggering back out the door.

Logan walked out of Brandy's Pantry, the local convenience store, with a bag of everything he could find on the shelves that wasn't pickled. The choices were slim. By spending just fifteen minutes inside the store, he had learned the many virtues of lard from two women in hats and become acquainted with the local minister, Pastor Elton Cooke, who had a debilitated pancreas and a legendary tenor singing voice.

An old, dusty red Dodge Spirit clattered appropriately through the parking lot like the soundtrack to the town of Barwell as Logan got into his vehicle. The black rental car was looking tired, showing the dirt from all the back roads. This whole town seemed to be made up of back roads, roads that didn't lead anywhere. The car wove through the town where time had been lost for decades, past fields dotted with silos and banks of red clay, and East towards the bridge.

"Well, what did she say?" Alexis was asking over the cellular waves.

"What they always say," Logan chortled. "Nothing. She said to find the one who hates this town more than I do."

"That's interesting," Alexis said nervously.

"It is," Logan mused, groping the wrapper off of a granola bar. "Probably just another riddle to get me distracted from the truth." He shoved the whole thing in his mouth.

"So you don't want me to look into it," Alexis stated, assuming the search was over.

"Oh of course I want you to look into it," Logan assured her, talking with his mouth full. "But I'm not going to waste another second with these nut jobs. I'm heading back out to the bridge."

"Why are you going back there?"

"I've been playing their game the whole time. They knew by doctoring the photos that I'd stop looking for the real evidence. And that's exactly what I did. Now that I'm thinking clearer... I want to go back to the scene of the crime and take a better look."

"Well, good luck with that."

"I'll take whatever I can get."

"Oh, oh Logan wait... I do have a little good news for you."

"Oh yeah?"

"I finally tracked down your luggage. It should be waiting for you at the hotel when you get back."

Logan pulled up to the stop sign opposite of Mitchel's Fill'n Station. He was astonished to see that the building was no longer rusted brown but looked brand new. It was white as snow. Even the parking lot had been repaved.

He replied with disbelief and confusion at the sight before him, "That *is* good news." A chime came through on his phone. "I gotta run, Lex. Keep me posted." He hung up and checked his screen and saw his boss's email address in his notifications. He shuddered.

Anders — awaiting your progress. Yes, this really is your last chance. Impress me, please.

Strauss

Clenching his fists around the steering wheel, he pulled past Mitchel's and on toward the crime scene.

Logan stood in the middle of the bridge, gazing down into the narrowest part of the Carrollton River, the water slapping the rocks along the shoreline. He shifted his weight, and the metal grating groaned slightly. Taking a small pencil and notebook from his jacket pocket, he tore a single sheet out and began sketching out his options.

"Why would a family man kill his entire family..." he mused to himself. "He wouldn't... unless he was crazy... like everyone else in this town." He knew he was going around in the same circle again. Then he scratched out what he had just written, redirecting his thoughts. "Innocent until proven guilty... What if we assume that he wouldn't? Then it was an accident or they're still alive..." He looked back at the road and then the concrete barrier fencing.

He recalled in slow motion his own near accident, racing toward the hairpin turn. The 15 mile per hour sign. The car skidding out of control. Dust and pine needles covering the hood.

"There's just no way he could have made that turn and accidentally went off. There's no way..." He folded the slip of paper in between his fingers over and over again. "He did it on purpose..." The rippling sound of the paper being rustled by the wind echoed for what seemed like miles. Logan's thoughts churned. He scratched out notes on the paper, and stood there for several more moments with the perplexing silence. Then he wrote one word in capital letters, and surveyed the riverbank with a new expression in his eyes. "So they are still alive." Logan startled as the pencil lead broke and flipped end over end through the grate into the water below. The distraction made him loosen his grip on the paper, and the wind stole it from his hands and it fluttered after the pencil like a caged bird, deep into the ravine.

"Moses William Benjamin Turner Underwood. They must have thought the more names they were given the more status they would have. This guy seemed to think he was King Daily of Barwell." Logan was 20 miles away in the neighboring town of Linsey, Va. He'd driven there on purpose to gain some perspective on the many twisted details he had uncovered so far this week, and felt some space might provide fresh ideas and maybe a decent meal. There was one establishment in Linsey that offered wi-fi, the Congress Café. He had gladly set up his work station in the corner booth and munched on club sandwiches and rice pudding while combing through the scans from Alexis of information connected to Thomas Capshaw and his family. The microfiche of newspaper articles and court documents relating to Capshaw and a corrupt District Attorney named Moses Underwood was beginning to aim light on the situation. And the food was helping too.

Moses Underwood apparently had been in a face-off with Sheriff Capshaw in 1987, the year before the sheriff and his family disappeared. All Logan could piece together was that the local law enforcement, headed by Capshaw, had flung Underwood's secret misdeeds into the public eye. And in the process, he had dethroned him from his imaginary seat of honor as one of the town's authorities. Capshaw uncovered a heaping sum of laundered money that Underwood had 'reappropriated.' The article stated that Underwood ended his life that same week.

All the other leads Alexis sent were deceased too.

Plaintive chords of a country song rang from the speakers as Logan arrived back at the hotel. He shook his head and settled within himself that no place whose radio stations played songs exclusively about farming, whiskey and lonely people in trucks could ever be considered home. He was more of a jazz man anyway.

As he was locking the car and walking towards the hotel, inside his room a black carry-on bag was being lifted from the floor and set onto the bed. When Logan entered the hotel lobby, he immediately noticed Daniel leering at him from behind a potted plant. Any other day, that kind of behavior would be considered normal, but Logan's *weirdo meter* was on high alert because of the dream he had had last night. Daniel stopped him, of course, to tell him that he had taken the liberty of putting his bag in his room for him. Then he asked about Logan's day, and Logan felt like he was stalling him for some reason.

Logan excused himself from his eccentric host and ascended the stairs. Just before he rounded the corner, a man exited his room and nonchalantly entered room 305 right as Logan reached the top of the staircase.

"Excuse me!" Logan called when he saw the man.

The man stopped but didn't speak or turn around, lingering in the doorway to the room next to Logan's.

"Is that your room?" Logan asked.

The man barely nodded yes.

"I hate to be rude but is there any way you could turn down your TV? These walls are paper thin… I've been having a hard time sleeping."

The man didn't say a word, just quickly went into his room and slammed the door. Logan shivered as he passed room 305, but shook it off and entered his own room.

The deadbolt clicked and the flimsy door wobbled open, and Logan wearily walked inside. He shut and locked the door behind him, and walked over to the suitcase on the bed.

"It's about time you showed up," he told his Samsonite. ZIP. The top of the carry-on flopped back against the bed with a thud. Logan stopped breathing.

A folded up paper he had never seen before was sitting on top of his clothes. He carefully reached out as if it were a poisonous snake. He exhaled forcefully, fearing he might lose his mind forever if he touched it. Unfortunately for him, his curiosity had always been stronger than his doubt.

Then the hotel phone clanged suddenly, making Logan seize with shock. His voice cracked like a teenager as he answered it.

"Hello?"

A deep male voice said briskly, "The Black Rooster. 3:00 PM. Bring the paper."

CLICK. Dial tone.

Logan placed the phone in its cradle. He looked again at the paper, and snatched it up. It was very old and had been ripped from something. He carefully unfolded it, and a flood of fear caught in his throat. The paper read,

Logan Anders, Chicago

CHAPTER EIGHT

Sadie unwrapped a package of strawberries after wearily trekking to three grocery stores to find what she was craving. Turning to place the fruit in the sink, she caught the pocket of her pants on a drawer handle and ripped them half way down her thigh, making her spill the berries across the floor. Angry tears gushed all over the place.

After allowing herself a moment to grieve her terrible luck, she got up the berries, cleaned the floor, threw away the pants and started over. Snuggling into some comfy sweats and flicking on the TV, she rinsed the berries off and made some hot chocolate as she searched for something to watch. Descending into the overstuffed chair that had become the only comfortable place to sit in the apartment, she caught her breath and rubbed her eyes. How many more weeks until this baby was due to arrive? She was only sure there were not enough.

She found a movie on TV and dug into her long awaited snack. But with the first bite, she suddenly spat it out, choking.

"Mleh!" she cried and sadly heaved herself up from her nest to throw the strawberries away. They tasted like ketchup. "What on earth! Now my hormones are making things taste weird? Listen, Baby Anders, you gotta stop messing with mommy. It's not fair." She dumped them down the disposal and gazed out the window behind the sink, hopeless at finding a shred of contentment in life and knowing she was being melodramatic about it.

An impression came over her. She shut off the water. Out the window, she saw the Ramson Building across Union, the cars sliding along the street, the sun setting. Something made her neck tingle with restive uneasiness.

She stood still, her eyes looking forward but her other senses on full alert. The TV was softly proclaiming the virtues of some kind of laundry product, and the smell of cocoa was wafting from the tin on the counter. She could still taste the strawberry-ketchup disaster. And as she adjusted her focus, she saw in the window a reflection of something behind her.

A matted, worn brown teddy bear was perched on top of the fridge, alongside several boxes of cereal and a canister of coffee. The lifeless toy seemed to be looking right at Sadie in the reflection of the window. She had never seen it before.

After silently, motionlessly trying to decide what to do for several minutes, she held her breath and forced herself to turn around to confront this uninvited creature lurking in the kitchen. *How very ridiculous*, she thought, looking it square in its plush face. A moment before it had seemed to be glaring at her with sinister intentions, but now, head on, it was harmless. But where had it come from?

Gathering the courage to approach the inanimate bear staring at her, she reached up and took him down, looking him in his black, glass eyes. He wasn't alive and spying on her, as her paranoia had insinuated. There was no danger here.

Still, there was no explanation, either.

Shaking her head, Sadie tried to calm her nerves and force the notion out of her head that she was being watched, or that this toy had been planted in her apartment to scare her. Why was that her first reaction anyway? She had no idea, but vowed never to let her eyes behold another episode of CSI.

Giving up on a relaxing evening of mindless TV and a bowl full of treats, Sadie shuddered and was suddenly very tired. The pressure of her husband being gone and not knowing if, when, or in what condition he would return was just exhausting. She crept into bed and fell asleep wondering whether her baby's eyes would turn out to be green like Logan's, or blue like her own.

The meeting place turned out to be a former pub whose brick face was painted black and whose heavy door was lacquered in crimson. It was nearly 100 years old and stood freely opposite a block of connected shops on the last stretch of the main road before it disappeared around the bend and into the mountains. There was a tackle shop, post office, a Dollar General, and a shoe repair store. They were all smudged with age, and a telephone pole was littered with posters and fliers from the local bands that played at the bar down the street. Country folks made their way back and forth across the street in their casual way, nodding to each other and minding their own business.

The Black Rooster

The Black Rooster's wide storefront windows all had the curtains drawn, and the roof was covered in wooden shingles that were blanketed with bright green moss. But the moss wasn't the only thing growing on the roof; there was also a tiny tree reaching skyward in an attempt to take up residence there.

Logan entered the tavern and had to blink to adjust his eyes to the dim light. Once he could see, he was impressed. He had not expected the inside of anywhere in Barwell to be as nice as this place.

Oddly enough though, there wasn't a single soul in sight.

"Hello?" Logan called. "Is anyone here?"

From the kitchen, a familiar waitress appeared. It was Missy from the Silver Diner. She looked him up and down and said, "Well, hey stranger. Canna help yew?"

"You... work here?" Logan surmised.

"The folks that own Silver Diner also own this place," she answered without looking away.

"Of course they do... makes perfect sense," Logan said, unsurprised at the incestuous nature of local businesses here.

Missy cocked her head to one side. "You didn't stop by this mornin' or yesterday. I put on a fresh pot ah coffee and everything."

"Yeah, uh, sorry about that," Logan sputtered. "Had a pretty rough start. Listen, are you open yet?"

"Absolutely. We're just a little slow this time ah day."

"I can see that," Logan confirmed, looking around the room.

"Would you like a table or a booth?" Missy showed Logan to a corner booth. "How's this?"

"It's fine, thank you," Logan said, sliding into the booth and accepting the menu from her.

"I'll give you a few minutes to decide," Missy clucked.

"Actually I'm meeting someone here. Could we hold off till he gets here?"

"Suit yourself. Let me know when you're ready." She walked back to the kitchen, but Logan didn't see her crack the door open again and peer through to watch him.

Two hours later, the restaurant was filling up for dinner

time. Missy was making her way around to each table and lighting a candle. Logan still sat alone, swirling a straw in his glass of ice water. When she reached his table, she lit the candle and lifted the water glass to sop up the condensation on the table. With disgust, she asked, "Would you like another glass of water?"

"No, I'm fine," Logan answered calmly.

Missy huffed. "Look, I don't mean to be rude, but you been here for hours. If you aren't gonna order anything, I'm gonna have to ask you to leave."

"Fine. I'll take the special." Logan was undeterred.

"The Black and Blue Medallions or the Peppercorn Encrusted Duck?"

"What's the difference," Logan said dismissively.

"The medallions is an eight ounce blackened filet topped off with blue…"

"No," he sighed. "What I meant to say is 'I don't care,' surprise me."

"As you wish," Missy huffed again.

She walked through the kitchen door and handed Logan's dinner order ticket to Daniel. "He said to surprise him," she added.

Daniel's expression was cold as stone. "Oh, he'll be surprised alright." He looked down at the ticket, and slammed it down on the ticket spike.

Logan's patience was wearing thin. His fingers rapped the top of the table while his feet fidgeted underneath. He took the slip of paper out of his jacket pocket and studied it once more. *Enough is enough!* He screamed in his mind, choking the life out of the paper and dropping its corpse onto the table.

He glared, seething, at the ball of paper, as an elderly hand reached down and set another piece of paper next to the first. "That's no way to treat evidence," said the person the hand belonged to, above Logan. He looked up. A stately gentleman, sharply dressed, stood before him. Each strand of his silver hair was swept back, each meticulously placed exactly where it ought to be.

Logan studied him for a moment. "It's a scrap of paper."

"...that I worked very hard to get for you," said the old man.

"It's a piece of paper," Logan growled.

"It's the key to pandora's box."

Logan twitched with anger. "I guess I am the only one who thinks it's strange that you people keep speaking in riddles." He snatched the second piece of paper from the table and opened it. It was his notes from the bridge, now weathered and slurred but still proclaiming one word: FAMILY. He looked up at the old man with his mouth gaping. "How did you get this?" he demanded.

Just then, the waitress walked up with a tray, holding the gentleman's usual drink.

"Thank you, my dear," the man said, accepting it from her.

"My pleasure," Missy replied, leaving.

The elderly man placed the drink in the center of the table and slipped into the booth opposite Logan. He looked at Logan with sudden fury. "You have no idea what you are messing with here," he accused.

"Why don't you enlighten me?" Logan countered.

"Some secrets aren't worth the cost of knowing... trust me."

"Trust you?" Logan said, hardly hiding his disgust. "You want me to trust you? I don't even know you... but as far as this evening is concerned, all you've done is waste my time." Logan rose to leave, but the man grabbed his arm to stop him.

"Sit down, son," he said firmly.

Logan had had about enough of people calling him 'son.' Nonetheless, he stole his arm back and eased back into the booth. The gentleman took the slip of paper and uncrumpled it, smoothing it out as much as possible on the table. He looked Logan right in the eyes. "As soon as I saw you I knew you reminded me of someone," he said condescendingly. "Does that ever happen to you? Man, it always drives me nuts until I figure it out... but I got it. You remind me of a kid I went to elementary school with. He was stupid too." He paused for effect, and Logan bristled. "One day after school we were goofing off and missed the bus, so we had to walk home. It was over five miles if we stayed on the sidewalk, so we took a shortcut through the woods. It wasn't too long before we came upon a massive hornets nest. The sound of all those bees rumbling inside was horrifying... absolutely horrifying. Guess what my little bone-headed friend decided to do? He took a handful of rocks from the trail and blasted the side of the nest."

Logan interrupted him. "Yeah, and he got stung. Great story."

"We both did," the man continued. "They didn't care that I didn't throw the rocks. They just stung me over and over and over again. Barely escaped with my life."

"I assume there's a moral to this story?" Logan blustered.

"It's never safe to assume anything, Mr. Anders," the old man said. "But let me tie it up for you with a nice little bow. You've missed the journalism bus and your career's teetering on the edge – if it hasn't already fallen into the toilet. And like every other arrogant reporter to roll into town, you thought we'd be your short cut back home to success and notoriety. But unlike my moronic little friend, you knew that the Capshaw case was a hornet's nest. You just didn't care." He slammed his fist on the table. "Now you've pissed off the bees... and you're not the only one that's going to get hurt."

He picked up the note he had brought with him. From the top of the paper to the bottom, he slowly wiped his fingers across it like a squeegee. Then he held it over the candle. "They told me you were hard-headed, but that was the understatement of the century... You're a fool." The flames caused the paper to glow. Faint puffs of smoke floated into the air as sections of the paper started to dry out.

"We've tried to be nice, but you've ignored every single warning. Plowed through every road block. Hell bent on getting your story." The paper burst into flames. "Losing your job not enough? What about good ole Mommy and Daddy? What about Sadie... the baby. What! What's it going to take, son?! What's it going to take to get you..." he trembled with nerve. "...to leave well enough alone?"

Missy had noticed the fire and run to the table. "Hey! You can't do that in here!"

Furious, Logan lunged across the table and socked the man across the face. The old man crumpled as his head spun to the side, reeling. Missy grabbed Logan's arm and screamed, "Don't just sit there, run!" and pointed him toward the back of the building.

Logan jumped to his feet and slipped away down the dark narrow hallway that led to the back exit. The man was rushing after him. Missy was knocking the burning paper off the candle and dowsing it with Logan's fourth glass of water, tamping it out with the bottom of the cup.

Like a linebacker, Logan plowed through the door... only to run right into Sheriff Crutcher. The officer thrust his knee into Logan's stomach, knocking the wind out of him. He yanked him back up from the ground and twisted Logan's arms behind his back. Then the sheriff slammed Logan chest first into the side of the patrol car.

Deputy Sheriff Smith was about to perish from the intensity. At his boldest, his voice carried little more impact than a kindergarten teacher. Trying his best to help, he frantically barked in a voice like a Yorkshire terrier, "Logan Anders, you have the right to..." Crutcher cut him off, thundering over him like a Doberman.

"You have the right to remain silent," the sheriff retched. "Anything you say can and will be used against you in the court of law... You have the right to an attorney..."

"I know my rights!" Logan blazed. "I have the right to not be arrested... when I haven't done anything wrong!" He noticed the elderly man about to slip away. "Hey! I bet your buddies down at the Lion's Club are really gonna get a kick out of this. This is some kind of a joke, right?!" he called after the strange man with flawless hair.

"No, Logan, this is very serious," the man replied, breathless.

"What did I ever do to you!" Logan screamed as the sheriff tried to force him toward the door of the car.

"I told you," the man said, wiping his forehead, "some secrets aren't worth the cost of knowing... Now it's time for you to go away."

He nodded to the sheriff, who clicked the first handcuff

on Logan's wrist. Without thinking, Logan fought back and surprised the officer, who grasped for his other arm to cuff him as Logan tried to outmaneuver his deadbolt grip.

He struggled with Crutcher for a few minutes, back and forth, grunting and burning, until the ironclad officer landed his knee in Logan's stomach. His phone fell out of his pocket and slammed on the ground, cracking the screen and going black, but Logan didn't notice with the wind having been knocked out of him. The effort made the sheriff pause to catch his breathe, and the useless deputy stood by practically wringing his hands. *You are NOT taking me down,* Logan seethed. Adrenaline triggered into his bloodstream, making his determination bulge all the more and wheeling a staggering right hook out of nowhere onto Crutcher's cheek. He lost his balance and the deputy immediately reached to help him, so Logan made a break for it around the corner of the building. The heavy but spry sheriff cursed and hustled himself into his cruiser, leaving poor Smitty behind in the alley.

Logan blazed down the street... dodging through alleyways... behind buildings to get away. He evaded the sheriff by hiding behind a dumpster until he went past. Then he went the opposite direction and headed away from town on foot.

CHAPTER NINE

$\mathcal{F}$all was coming early in Chicago. The pristine streets were full of urbanites enjoying the weather, taking in the sunshine and reveling in the magic that only descends on a city when the temperatures pluck imperceptibly at the pedestrians and the sun is not too bright, and not too hidden. The Ghirardelli ice cream shop buzzed with customers all rushing for their first hot chocolate of the season, and the Magnificent Mile bustled with hired vehicles servicing the wealthy shoppers in their quest for new fall fashions. Red leaves were blinking in the breeze along Union Street.

High above the street, the Anders apartment wasn't so serene. Sadie was frantically throwing items into a suitcase. She had made up her mind she was going to find her husband, and Francis had tried to no avail to reason with her.

"Something's wrong. He could be hurt or worse, I don't know, but I have to find out what's going on," Sadie told her friend.

"You know you can't fly!" Francis protested. "You're eight months pregnant!"

"I wasn't planning on it," Sadie assured. "And thanks for reminding me that I'm pregnant. I almost forgot," she retorted sarcastically.

"Well, if you were counting on me driving, you'd better think again!" Francis shrieked, almost in tears at her friend's senselessness. And Francis never shed tears for any reason.

Sadie stopped and looked at her with serious eyes. "Come on, Fran. What if it were Travis? What if Travis were missing?"

Francis just looked away, knowing she was right. Not to be outdone by a loopy pregnant lady, her fearless inner combatant rose to the challenge, and she got up from the couch to help Sadie pack. "Well," she said slowly, garnering control of the situation, "What is taking you so freaking long? Do I need to do everything around here? Give me that bag, you go get your makeup case and a toothbrush."

Sadie looked at her and her lip trembled. When she didn't get a response, Francis looked up and saw Sadie about to lose it. Francis started shaking her head and backing away. "Oh, no you don't. Hold it together, Anders. I can't handle your emotional rollercoaster!" Sadie burst into a mixture of laughter and tears, collapsing into a chair. Francis let out a shaky breath, satisfied that she had avoided too deep of a 'girl moment' and was now fully in the driver's seat of this recon mission.

"Go, hop to it," she barked at Sadie, who wiped her

cheeks and nodded an appreciative pout at her friend for being strong for her before disappearing into the tiny bathroom to collect her things. Francis folded the last of the clothes into the suitcase and surveyed the cramped apartment. She let out a low grumble and insisted to herself, "There is *no way* I am driving. We are taking a train."

The sun was setting, washing the landscape in an amber glow. Warm colors were dappling the trees as harvest time approached. The mountains reached and fell along the horizon, and made Logan miss the Chicago skyline. The city had never felt like a lonely concrete jungle to him, but this lush, ancient wilderness he had found himself wandering was silent and unknown. They both seemed to hold more secrets than one man could discover in a lifetime. To a reporter, it was a seductive mirage of endless intrigue.

Logan was hiking up a steep incline, the handcuffs jangling from one wrist. He crested the hill and started down the other side, not sure where he was going, but as he looked below he slowed to a halt. His thoughts stopped. He stood there for a while, silent, taking in the view. A wide lake spread out before him, low in the valley. The jagged mountains in the distance were blue and gray, flanking the still water for miles. A disreputable looking farmhouse stood on the seam of the mountains and the lowland. It had been abandoned for a long time, but Logan could make out a motley cat chasing something in the grass nearby.

Mustering a second wind, he ran along the tree line where

the fireflies were starting to come out and across the open field, scaring off the cat and stepping onto the sagging porch steps. There was a large wicker peacock chair, gray and tattered, that stood aging on the porch. It had been exposed to the weather for a long time, and seemed if it were to be touched it would collapse into a pile of dust with a dry *poof.* The window glass was gone, the railings were gone, the paint was almost gone, and several floor boards were gone too. Treading carefully, Logan dismissed the urge to test the integrity of the chair and walked past it to the door. The knob was barely connected, and the door swung open.

He walked through the hallway, slowly and quietly, his heart hammering with uncertainty. Personal belongings that had been left long ago still sat strewn about. There had been a fire here. The wall paper was black with soot in some places and part of the floor was missing near the kitchen. Tiny antique appliances were crammed along one wall, and the missing window had allowed crackling brown leaves to litter the sink and counter. Logan rifled through the cabinets, finding a vintage can of Campbell's soup in a drawer, some wooden spoons, a screwdriver, and a deceased bat. He went to leave through the back of the kitchen, only to find that the steps were missing.

A faded sense of wonder crept over him as he jumped to the ground and politely closed the door behind him. He was exhausted and had no idea how he was going to get home. Even after walking for the last two hours and his nerves coming back to their senses, he had alighted on fewer answers to this whole mystery than he had a hold of when he arrived.

He shook his head as he walked over to a big barn, considering it's placement in his stack of options for overnight accommodations. The large door moaned as Logan turned it on its hinge and opened it for the first time in who knew how long.

A high loft surrounded the ceiling, and a few cats scurried away when the light reached them from the open door. Logan surveyed the situation dubiously before swinging the barn door shut. He walked along the stalls, hoping to find a stack of saddle blankets or even a hay bale to rest on. At the end of the barn, in the last stall, an old pickup truck was parked, rusty and unused. He almost cried with relief and climbed onto the big bench seat, spent. He lay looking up through the truck window at the dusky evening sky through cracks in the barn roof, hoping no one would find him, and fell fitfully to sleep.

Once again, Ron Mitchel's pickup truck approached the Mineral Pallet Company, lit dimly even with the black country night all around. This time he killed the lights and pulled into the shadows, backing in, and waited with a full view of the highway. His reddish beard was almost gray now, but oddly his thin dark hair was still the color it had always been. He had a sort of calico coloring to him and his hazel eyes seemed to take on any color you decided they were. He pulled at his whiskers and thought of his grandkids, who were always complaining about his beard scritch-scratching their tender faces. He checked the rearview mirror every sixty seconds for twelve minutes straight, calm and ready.

The green Taurus came over the rise from town, and the headlights went dark. A few moments later, the car coasted into the lot and its convenient shadows, right next to Mitch. They stared at each other in their vehicles for a brief moment, before rolling down the windows to talk.

"Hey," Michelle Claridge hissed.

"Hey," he replied.

"What do we do now, Mitch?"

"You better have some kinda plan ready when he shows up at 'dat precinct... 'cause they gonna bring 'em in... that's f'shore."

"The police are already looking for him. But this guy is slick. He could be hiding anywhere, and if Butch finds him, he's a goner." The D.A. shuddered at the thought.

Mitch thumbed his sideburns and looked out at the road. "I don't know the law like you do but somethin' needs done, or Butch is go' get to 'em first."

The woman looked at the lumber yard beyond her windshield. Her nerves were about to short circuit from the pressure. She let out a shaky sigh and looked back at Mitch in the dark. "I think I know what will work," she finally admitted. "Barwell isn't that big... there's only one place we haven't looked yet."

*   *   *

Ping. Peck. Scratch. A black chicken was hunting for bugs in the exposed engine cavity of the truck. Minding its own business, it hopped around and leisurely snacked on the insects abiding in the unused vehicle. The bird made its way up into the empty windshield space and looked sideways at the sleeping human. Then it wiggled its way inside and landed squarely in Logan's lap. When his eyes flew open to black feathers rustling in his face and tiny claws on his legs, he screamed and thrashed at the evil creature that was attacking him, scaring the chicken senseless and kicking the dash so hard his foot hurt. The bird shrieked and toddled and fluttered its way out of the truck window, running away as fast as it could.

Logan sat, blinking, heaving, trying to remember what he was doing there. He gulped, and his throat was sorely dry. He rubbed his burning eyes and laid his head back on the seat, trying to calm down. *The barn, yes*, he remembered. *Shelter. What time is it?* He opened his eyes again and it seemed to be dark still. It must be night. He noticed the glove box was open, which he must have kicked in his squabble with the chicken.

Not one to take someone else's personal affects for granted, he pulled the contents out and began sorting through it. An old photo slipped from the pile and landed in a dried puddle of oil that had soaked into the floorboard. He pulled it out and laid it on the dashboard. It was a family picture of a mother, father, and son. Logan's head suddenly cleared, and the hair on the back of his neck stood erect. He rifled through the papers from the glove box and found a registration paper with THOMAS CAPSHAW listed as the vehicle's owner.

MARSHAL HUNTER   LEAH SPRADLIN

Shock, then realization washed over Logan as he accepted that he was sitting in the very truck from the accident he was here to discover.

He picked up the photo again and held it up to the faint moon light. He ran his eyes over the faces in the photo over and over. He turned the photo over to find something faintly written there, but he couldn't tell what it said. He moved the picture closer and closer to his face, almost until he couldn't focus on it anymore, willing the letters to straighten up and appear legible.

Then a crash behind him made his blood freeze. He whipped his head around to see the barn door open and two silhouettes coming toward him in the moonlight, weapons drawn.

"Freeze Anders!" Sheriff Crutcher screamed. "Get your hands up!"

"Get your hands up now!" an unfamiliar deputy shouted.

Like a deer in headlights, Logan didn't know what to do.

"Get out of the truck and slowly turn around," the sheriff said. Logan didn't notice he was still grasping the picture as he held his handcuffed arm up in the air while opening the door with his free hand.

Not satisfied with how quickly Logan was moving, the sheriff practically ripped the door off its hinges and aggressively yanked Logan from the truck. "Are you deaf or stupid?! Get out of the truck!" He was screaming wildly. He slammed Logan to the ground and yanked his arms behind him, firmly cuffing his other wrist. The deputy, an officer conversely as capable as Smith had been underwhelming, had a gun trained on Logan as the sheriff dispelled every ounce of his revenge onto the reporter. A cloud of dust swirled up around them like a baseball player sliding into home plate, making Logan choke and wheeze miserably. The sheriff ripped the photo from Logan's hand, and the two officers dragged their perpetrator to the patrol car, tossing him gruffly into the back seat and nodding breathlessly at each other with satisfaction.

Black, patent leather high heels clicked down the hallway of the police station, stopping right outside the interrogation room. A battered Logan sat uncomfortably on a cold metal chair that was bolted to the floor. He was wearing a grey jumpsuit. As the door opened, Logan looked up and was introduced to the owner of the high heels, District Attorney Michelle Claridge. She was a trim woman in her fifties, with fading blonde hair pinned back neatly and bright, big eyes. A severe, nervous expression ruled her angular face.

"Finally found time to meet with me," he smirked relentlessly.

"If I recall correctly," the D.A. responded coolly, "You're the one that stood me up."

"Touche."

"Can I get you anything to drink?" D.A. Claridge asked

with corporate pleasantness. "Coffee… water… um, coffee?"

"You can get me the lawyer I've already asked for three times."

"Relax," she cooed, tilting her head to one side. "I wouldn't think of violating your rights." She walked over to the two-way mirror and tapped on the glass. "We're going to need some privacy," she told the unseen observer.

A speaker in the wall crackled to life. "You got it."

Concern washed over Logan's face. The D.A. walked back around to the other side of the table and slid a folder across to him. Logan eyeballed it without touching it.

"Open it," she said softly.

Logan reached across and pulled the flap up. Inside was a large black and white mug shot of the burly man he had encountered at the filling station.

"Recognize him?" she asked.

"Yeah…" Logan replied, confused. "I met him a couple days ago out at Mitchel's Fill'n Station. He's lovely." As he flipped through a few pages of a report, the D.A. began to explain.

"His name is Bill Underwood," she said, wandering around the room as she spoke. "Everyone around here calls him Butch. His rap sheet is longer than the prison tats running down his hairy back. Spent time for everything from shoplifting to armed robbery, drug possession with intent to distribute, assault and battery, you name it…"

"What connection does he have to Moses Underwood?" Logan asked, peering at her sideways.

Claridge paused and said simply, "Moses was Butch's father. He was even more diabolical than his son."

"I get it, he's bad news," Logan interjected. "Why are you telling me this?"

"He wants you dead," she said, facing away.

"Tell him to get in line," Logan retorted.

Claridge whipped around and looked at him. "You have no idea what you're dealing with," she warned.

"I think you have no idea who you're dealing with," he said, meeting her cold gaze. "It takes a lot more than a night in jail to intimidate me."

She silently faced off with Logan, as memories filled his mind of the threats and close calls he had encountered as a journalist. Being the most brazen reporter on staff had been his greatest pride, but had put him in the company of four of the most evil criminals in his hometown. He was realizing that a lot of his bulletproof attitude was caused by the trust in the full extent of the law that was behind him, but here at the foot of a surly mountain range, he had no support and no backup. The nearest reliable colleague was 613 miles northwest in Illinois, if there was one. He willfully ignored the impending notion that he might truly be alone. "This mountain boy might be big but where I'm from we got big shoulders and lots of crime. He doesn't scare me," Logan vowed falsely.

"You and everyone you care about are in serious danger," Claridge told him, humorless. "And the second you publish this story, there will be no place for you to hide. He's extremely good at hunting people down and killing them."

"How should I know you aren't protecting him?"

"Because I know first hand how evil he is," she snapped, her voice crackling.

"Or maybe, like everyone else in this town, you are a part of the cover up – trying to run me out of town before I can expose the truth."

"There is no conspiracy!" She was quickly losing her cool. "You've read the files. Back in '88, Sheriff Thomas Capshaw accidentally nailed the kingpin of one of the largest meth labs on the east coast. A bunch of warehouses on the edge of town… out by Mitchel's Fill'n Station…"

"There's nothing out there but open fields and woods," Logan countered, making a mental note of the meth lab. He had in fact not read any files.

"You didn't see 'em because Butch had them burned to the ground when the Feds started their investigations."

"And there's nothing in the police reports about a fire," Logan said viciously.

"Because the fire didn't take place until a month after the disappearances..."

Logan slammed the papers down onto the table to silence her. "Let me save you some time," he growled. "Capshaw responded to the domestic dispute call that was a couple of miles away from the warehouse. No one really knows what happened, but shots were fired and a witness reported hearing someone yelling 'I know where you live. I know where you live! You're a dead man! You hear me!'"

The D.A. interrupted him. "Everyone knows that Butch killed that family... but there was no way to prosecute him. Every hope of evidence was lost in the fire."

Logan's nerves were pulsating. "Which fire? The warehouse or the courthouse?"

The D.A. seemed to be rattled for a second. "What difference does it make?" she asked quickly.

"The difference between the truth and a lie is in the details," Logan answered, leaning back and folding his arms with a knowing grin.

"There were no witnesses and all the evidence was destroyed. You have no details," she assured him, regaining her confidence.

"So you're telling me to let sleeping dogs lie... is that it?"

"I'm telling you that some answers aren't worth the cost of knowing." She eyed him with a hundred layers of meaning.

Every one of Logan's nerves was standing at attention. Softer, she continued. "Believe it or not, I'm trying to help you. And I will help you if you'll let me." Her hushed tone made Logan look at her.

"I must be the luckiest man alive," he said gleefully, folding his hands behind his head. "It's not every day one gets arrested for no apparent reason, and then finds out that the head prosecutor wants to help prove he's innocent. So what does that make you? My guardian angel?"

Pissed off, the D.A. stormed around the table and got right in Logan's face. "I am *no one's* angel. I'm Satan's mean big sister when it comes to Bill Underwood," she spat. "He was never more treacherous to anyone than he was to me." She turned her back to Logan and seemed to be baiting his curiosity. He waited for the silence to nudge her, and it worked. "Bill Underwood was my husband."

No way... he thought. "No way," he repeated aloud.

She peeked over her shoulder to make sure he was waiting for her to go on. "He beat the snot out of me, Anders. For three years. I wish I could say he was an alcoholic, but he was stone sober. He was just so mean and vicious. I... I... I couldn't give him what he wanted, and he hated me for it. So I don't take crap from anyone, anymore." She either realized she was volunteering information or she was offering a hoax of vulnerability. Logan couldn't tell, but that was it, and the vault sealed again.

Composing herself, she turned and said, "I may not look

like the devil to you, but I am the only one standing between you and hell, Logan. So I suggest that you shut your mouth and start listening." She backed away and straightened her blazer. "There is only one way out of this mess alive."

Logan looked straight ahead and said, "What's that?"

"Plead guilty."

Logan stared at her, incredulous. "Plead guilty? Guilty to what? You haven't even charged me yet!"

"Tomorrow morning when you stand before the judge... you are going to plead guilty and accept whatever punishment comes down." She sounded strangely friendly, but she wouldn't look him in the eye now.

"You've got to be kidding."

"No, Logan, I am very serious. You have no choice but to..."

"I do have a choice! I am not guilty of anything here!"

"Suit yourself," she said, suddenly icy again. "It's your funeral." After a beat of silence, she collected her file and moved towards the door.

"This is absurd!" Logan called after her. "I know my rights and I haven't done anything wrong. I want to see my lawyer *now!*"

She paused before exiting. "I'm sorry you feel that way."

"I'm getting to the bottom of this if it's the last thing I ever do," he promised solemnly.

Coldly, softly, she reminded him of her advice. "No, you hear me... plead guilty, Anders, or you're as good as dead." Without giving him time to argue, the door clicked behind her.

Shafts of moonlight illuminated Logan's cell as he sat with his head in his hands, exhausted and worried. A guard clinked his keys along the jail bars and stopped at his cell.

"Hey!" he called gruffly. "Wake up!"

Logan slowly came to his feet as the guard unlocked the cell. He was led to an old pay phone around the corner. "You got one minute," the guard said severely.

Logan dialed and waited as the phone rang over and over. Then he heard Sadie's voice, and relief swept over his whole body... wait, it was just her voicemail. Sorrow flooded his weary soul once again.

Hi! This is Sadie. I'm sorry I missed your call, but if you leave a detailed message, I will call you back as soon as I can. Have a great day!

"Honey, it's me..." Logan found himself suddenly without words. "I've got to make this quick, but I just wanted to say you were right... about everything. And that I'm sorry... I'm so sorry..."

The guard tapped him in the back with his billy stick.

"Hurry it up."

Slowly, reluctantly, Logan said what he didn't want to admit to his wife. "You deserve someone so much better than me... someone who will care for you, who will listen to you... and love you. Listen... I need you to know that if anything happens to me... if I do not make it home..."

"That's enough," the guard commanded, grabbing the phone and slamming it back into the receiver.

"Hey!" Logan couldn't believe it. "I wasn't done yet!"

The guard didn't say anything, just shoved Logan back down the hall to his cell. One last forceful shove sent Logan stumbling backwards. His head smacked the wall and he slid down each of the cinder blocks until he bounced harshly off the tarnished metal rim of the toilet. The guard uncaringly locked the door and continued on about his business.

Logan crawled off the floor and into the bed, his head seeping blood onto the pillow. He looked at the ceiling and moaned in pain, and his eyes fluttered shut.

CHAPTER TEN

*C*LANG. The loud sound of the cell door opening caused Logan to jolt awake.

"Get up," the guard muttered.

Logan struggled to get to his feet as a massive pounding headache hammered off a trill of pain through his skull. He lost his balance and sat back down on the bed.

"I said get up. Now get to your feet," the guard shouted.

"I'm trying... I can't stand for some reason," Logan said, rubbing the back of his head. His body felt like it weighed a thousand pounds.

The guard impatiently grabbed him by the back of the neck and pulled him to his feet. "See, I knew you could do it," he sneered. He motioned for Logan to reach out his arms, and firmly shackled his hands and feet before shoving him out the door and down the hall.

A small group of reporters was waiting outside the courthouse for Logan's arrival. A couple of TV vans were parked on the sidewalk with the satellites raised high in the air.

Sheriff Crutcher's cruiser pulled up to the curb as Logan peered anxiously through the window. The door flung open, and the sheriff ushered Logan down the sidewalk. Various reporters asked questions in rapid fire succession, but he ignored them. He lowered his head and tried to cover his face as best he could.

The traditional dark wood courtroom was completely empty of spectators. The sheriff guided Logan to the defendant's chair, yanking the shackles to make him comply.

"Sit... Good boy," the sheriff glared. Then he walked to the front of the room and stood with his arms crossed.

From the rear of the room, the D.A. made a pointed entrance and made her way past the prosecutor's table. "Good morning, Mr. Anders," she said brightly. Logan rolled his heavy eyes. "I trust you got a good night's rest." Logan remained silent. "You know it's rude not to speak when spoken to," she admonished, growing impatient.

"I thought I had the right to remain silent," Logan stated calmly.

"That you do," she conceded. "That you do."

Logan noticed himself descending into the arms of an uncanny sense of helplessness. No logic could be made of the situation he was finding himself in, and he was beginning to fear that there really was no way out of this mess. He had always been in control of his surroundings. Even when in compromising circumstances when it had been necessary to invent his own outcome, he had the freedom to chart his own course out of whatever mess he had created. Over the past several years with the Chronicle, he had chased down the most aggressive stories in the Chicago-land area and landed himself in some ironic Holmes-and-Watson style predicaments, but his wits were no match for this obscure town where nothing followed the bounds of the law or natural society.

Everyone in the courtroom seemed to be unworried, and sort of relaxed, Logan noted. Was no one concerned that justice may not prevail for him? Were they all in on this cover up? Was he out of his mind for expecting the law to protect him? There were no solid truths to align these questions with, only endless variables that offered no reassurance.

The sheriff snapped to attention. "All rise," he called out.

An elderly man dressed in a flowing black robe entered. Logan recognized him as the same man he had met at the tavern the long night before. Like mountain goats preparing to butt heads, their necks stiffened, and their eyes locked.

The Sheriff spoke up. "Department One of the Superior Court is now in session. The Honorable Leland Hawthorne is presiding."

Logan struggled to get back to his feet, but the shackles snagged on the chair, causing him to fall back into the seat.

Sheriff Crutcher was disgusted. "Please be seated."

Perched high above the floor, Judge Hawthorne peered down his long nose for several silent moments. The clerk sat to the right of the bench, having seemingly appeared out of nowhere.

The Judge spoke. "This is a preliminary hearing. Do you understand what that means, Mr. Anders?"

Logan responded with unmasked spite in his voice. "Under normal circumstances, I would say that I do, Your Honor. But I think we can all agree that these are not normal circumstances."

The Judge immediately took offense. "Well, for the sake of clarity and for your edification, let me spell it out for you. At a preliminary hearing, the judge decides whether the defendant gets to have a trial or not. And based on my understanding of the evidence already presented… I have to say I'm rather inclined not to proceed to trial. See, the tax payers really don't like their dollars wasted. And you… sir… are an absolute waste of money, space, time, energy. Fill in the blank with whatever you like."

"I object!" Logan blustered. "There has been no evidence presented!"

"Over-ruled," the Judge said with finality.

* * *

At the Barwell train station, Sadie and Francis were walking into the restroom when Francis stopped cold, staring over Sadie's shoulder.

"What are you looking at?" Sadie wondered.

Her friend squinted. "Is that Logan?"

Sadie turned around and followed Francis's gaze toward an old box TV mounted to the wall of the train station. A video clip was airing of Logan being escorted into the courthouse in handcuffs, hunkering down in his jacket as reporters grilled him with questions.

As the newscaster came back on to continue the report, Sadie was so paralyzed with shock and confusion she didn't hear anything else coming from the TV speaker.

"What in the world is going on?!" Francis exclaimed. Her tone had turned rigid. Sadie was too stunned to shush her friend's outburst. "Sadie have you talked to him? Why is he in custody?" The questions were unmet with answers. She paused to read the captions at the bottom of the screen, scanning the headlines to catch a glimpse of the situation. Sadie just tried to keep breathing. "Hey, what happened with that guy?" Francis cawed to a passing stranger carrying a tray of drinks and forcing his attention to the TV. He shrugged and walked away.

Francis stormed over to a station attendant, invading his personal space entirely, demanding his attention. Sadie just stood, motionless, as the news moved along to the next dribble of local drama. After a heated dispute with the attendant about his awareness of society and where he could shove his departure schedules, Francis stomped back to Sadie. "We are going down to that courthouse, and we are taking a flamethrower to the place if they don't tell us exactly what is going on here," Francis threatened. Simultaneously, she reaffirmed her own confidence and scared Sadie to pieces. Francis saw her face go limp with fear. "Hey!" she screamed. Sadie looked at her and started to cry. "Hey!!! Stop it, just stop. Don't get all emotional. I don't want to smack you!" Francis said, half worried and half determined to remain in control of the situation. Her cheeks were flushed. "Go pee," she commanded Sadie. "We are going to go get Logan back."

Judge Hawthorne looked at Sheriff Crutcher and directed him to get Logan to his feet. The bailiff jerked him forcefully out of his chair.

The Judge cleared his throat. "Let the record show that Mr. Anders has waved his right to a trial by a jury of his peers."

Logan was stunned. "What?! Wait a minute! I didn't wave anything!"

"Mr. Logan Anders, II, you are charged with multiple counts of interfering with an ongoing police investigation, breaking and entering, destruction of property, resisting arrest, assaulting an officer, and tampering with evidence. How do you plea?"

Logan clenched his jaw. "Not guilty, Your Honor."

The Judge slammed the gavel dramatically. "Let the record show that Mr. Anders has also been charged with perjury."

"Hey!" Logan screamed, losing his cool once and for all. "I don't know what you're trying to pull here, but this is an outrage. This is an outrage! You, sir, are the liar. You are! And your sheriff, the deputy, the D.A., and everyone else in this psychotic town!"

Stark silence descended over the courtroom. Shame settled over Logan as he realized that he had over done it. His outburst had ruffled the judge's feathers.

Judge Hawthorne rose, smoldering, from his chair. "Due to the defendant's deteriorating mental stability, the court sees no reason to delay sentencing." SLAM! The gavel fell again. "Mr. Anders, you are hereby sentenced to ten years in prison without parole and with no opportunity for reduction of the sentence based on good behavior or time served..." SLAM! SLAM! "You will immediately be remanded to the county jail, until which time arrangements have been made to transfer you to a state penitentiary." SLAM! The judge wiped spittle from his mouth with one hand, and carefully ran his other hand over his flawless white hair. "Case dismissed."

As the impact echoed through the courtroom, a tidal wave of disbelief came crashing over Logan. Reality was suspended as he was hauled away by the sheriff, who glowered at him without mercy.

Frantically, he tried to withstand the beckoning chasm of fear by calmly counting the portraits he passed in the hallway as he was led toward the doors. He said nothing. The rectangle of light at the end of the hall was surely where this nightmare was going to end, and he was going to wake up. His mind called a hundred different plays, but none of them included going back to jail.

Outside the courthouse, a cab pulled up to the curb a few blocks away. Sadie exited and rushed as best she could down the sidewalk, with Francis clamoring behind her.

Sadie saw a defeated Logan being pulled across the courthouse commons toward the row of patrol cars and news vans parked on the street. She tried to yell for her husband, but her voice failed her. She waved her arms in desperation, but Logan was unaware. She kept running. "Wait!!" She shouted, growing more hysterical with every step Logan and the sheriff closed toward the car.

Out of the corner of her pooling eyes, Sadie saw a bald, burly man step out from a building across the street from the courthouse. She looked and saw him pull a revolver out of his belt and aim it at her husband.

"Logan!! Wait!!" She screamed frantically. He finally heard her, and she locked eyes with him, still a block away.

"Sadie! Sadie!" He immediately tried to break away from the Sheriff, but the officer grabbed him and shoved him into the sidewalk. Sadie still desperately tried to reach him.

Logan looked up at his wife from the pavement, and suddenly saw himself watching his parents car burn from the same angle. "Sadie!!!" He yelled with everything he had. Then the sheriff stepped away from Logan. He was so worn from fighting and so shocked at the appearance of his wife that he didn't question why he was free, but leapt up and started toward his wife.

"Logan!!" Sadie cried, as two shots rang out from the barrel of the revolver pointed at him. Struck in the chest, Logan went back down hard on the cement. Sadie reached him and collapsed to the ground beside him, screaming his name.

Francis caught up and dropped next to her friend. "My God, Sadie!!" she screamed. "Logan! Are you alright? Are you hit? Somebody call 911!"

EMT's rushed a stretcher through the ER doors with a bang, barking orders, and vital statistics. Sadie lay on the stretcher. The paramedics shouted about saving the child. "The baby is breached. We have to do an emergency c-section, now!"

Francis charged right behind the stretcher, completely ignoring the threats of the rescue squad that she couldn't accompany their patient unless she was immediate family. Her face was red with fury, but she made her tone stay neutral and under control, talking to Sadie all along, in case her friend heard her and could somehow be comforted.

Sadie was barely conscious. Different faces, masked and sterile, came in and out of focus as she looked through her useless eyes. Eventually, she thought she saw Logan's parents hovering over her, looking worried. She was barely awake, but the confusion was frantic, and the pain was agonizing. She pleaded with them, or the apparition of them, desperate to know what happened to Logan.

As the fog of anesthesia overtook her, they simply answered, "Everything is going to be okay. Everything ... is... going... to be... okay..." and Sadie's consciousness slowly collapsed. That's when the dreams started, flashbacks of things she had never experienced.

*   *   *

The owls had watched silently as flashlights and frantic footsteps scuffled below on the road. The sudden assembly of heavy-booted men and their trucks crunching gravel and hustling about in the dark had unnerved a few nocturnal animals who sputtered their disgust at the interruption. A little boy cried as he was thrust from one vehicle to another. His parents whispered concise words to the booted men, climbed in beside their son, and thrust a piece of paper with a name and city scribbled on it into someone's hands. Then they were driven across the bridge with the headlights off and nothing but the moon lighting the way.

Two men redirected the truck to face the river, and another was up the road near the hairpin turn, keeping an eye out for unwanted headlights. The truck was left in neutral, and the two men stepped around to the back bumper and looked at each other solemnly before grabbing hold of the rear

150

bumper and pushing with all they had. They both caught their breath when the truck took out a small tree, almost getting stuck, on its way down the steep river bank. It thundered toward the water and plowed right in, sending tremors through the still night and causing the owls to leave their branches with a huff of indignity.

The third conspirator jogged back from up the road, and they quickly but carefully got in their trucks and parked in the trees along the bridge road, deep enough to not be noticed in the dark but within view of the scene. They all traded nervous glances as the woods became silent again.

Ninety seconds later, a brigade of emergency vehicles rounded the bend and came screeching to a halt, expelling the nightlife once again from their dwellings. The three men in boots left their trucks and joined the rescue crew swarming in the road. The police chief was giving hushed but firm orders to a young deputy, and paramedics were gathering to hear when the oldest of the booted men walked right through the circle of them and approached the chief. He explained with a grim tremble that if Sheriff Capshaw was going to make it out of town, they had better turn in a good alternative story to the newspaper. Either that or get comfortable with the idea of Bill Underwood slitting all their throats. The chief crossed his arms and listened, not used to taking input but knowing there was no room for ego here. He thought for a moment and then smoothed his hand over his immaculate hair that was graying on the sides.

"Thank you Mitch," he sighed. "Get Janet Hess from The Porch Dweller on the phone, she's the only one you can trust. Tell her Hawthorne sent you, and she'll print whatever you tell her to." Ron Mitchel took a deep breath and gave Chief Hawthorne a grateful nod. He ran back to his jeep in the woods and rumbled back past the company of rescue workers to get into town and use a phone.

CHAPTER ELEVEN

*L*ogan's eyes opened for the second time to a cell-like room where he was completely alone. As he woke up, he realized he was in some kind of very deeply quiet hospital suite, and his chest was aching. The walls were an aged shade of green and empty of decorative effort, and there seemed to be no lamp or fixture from which the diluted, ambient light originated from. If there were a room more depressing in the world, Logan didn't want to know of it. He lifted his arms to try to remove the invisible herd of circus elephants from on top of him, but found he couldn't move his arms or legs. Slowly, he realized he was fully tethered to the bed he was laying on. A primal fear like he had never experienced before oozed over him, like a broken over-easy egg yolk. He began tugging so violently that the bed shuddered several inches across the floor, but it didn't do him any good; he was trapped. A warmth of panic descended over him, and he swallowed hard, trying not to freak out. An IV bag hung next to him, and the tube snaked under his sleeve and disappeared somewhere up his arm. There was no telling what was pumping through his blood stream.

"Help me!!!" He cried out at the top of his lungs. "Help me, somebody, please!" But his words fell mute... mute because his mouth was muzzled.

The door opened. All Logan could see behind the drawn medical curtain was a pair of black patent leather pumps walking in and closing the door behind them. Logan stiffened, and his blood turned cold. The shoes clicked around the curtain and District Attorney Michelle Claridge appeared in the dark, sterile room.

Logan winced in pain with each slow pulse of his aching heart.

The D.A. just looked at him for a moment. Her eyes were missing the steel and grit from before. She moistened her lips and said, "Congratulations, Anders. You made it. You're alive." Logan didn't respond, so she continued. "I am here to tell you what you came to learn... but first, I need you to behave." She came closer and examined his eyes till she was confident that he would comply. "Are you going to behave, Anders?"

He lowered his eyes in reluctant submission. She loosened the straps on the muzzle and lifted it over his head.

"What are you doing here?" Logan stammered, barely audible with infuriation. *Oh no... Sadie.* She was the last thing he remembered seeing. "What happened to Sadie?"

"She is nearby. She is safe."

He let out a shallow exhale of relief, followed by a gasp as another fearful anxiety struck him. "The baby?!"

Claridge took her time before answering, carefully calculating the right answer. "I'm afraid I don't know."

"I need to see her!"

"I know… and you will. You were just x-rayed a few minutes ago to check for residual damage from the impact of the bullet. Once the doctor clears you, I will arrange for you to see your wife."

Bullet? Logan had no idea what she was talking about. "So why am I in a straight jacket like a lunatic?"

Her demeanor softened slightly. "It's for your own safety, Logan. We knew you wouldn't listen… You'd resist or run or put up a fight… if we did it any other way."

She crossed the foot of the bed and offered him a sip of water from a straw inside a cup on the bedside table. Logan, unsure of any reason to argue because nothing could make any less sense than it already did, obeyed. In a moment of stoic humility, the D.A. held the cup and lifted Logan's head while he drank from it gratefully. He couldn't bear to look her in the eyes, and she didn't speak. In a strange room as silent as a grave, this egotistical reporter and an equally proud government official were calling a truce, both simply worn out from the day. She took a shaky breath and tried to center herself. "Logan, your presence in Barwell has caused quite a stir, but not for the reasons you might think. We knew you were coming. Well, we didn't know *you* were coming, but… Let me fill you in on a little bit of local history.

"I was married to Butch, as I told you. Unfortunately for me, and to make a long story short, I married him when I was very young because that's the sort of thing that happens in rural towns where there is little to do. I told him as soon as I found out I was pregnant. We got married even though I barely knew him six months, and I had no idea who he really was. And by the time the honeymoon was over…" she shuddered… "The baby was gone. Instead, I ended up with a bitterly angry husband. You can't imagine the guilt I felt, the guilt I feel even today. But even as young as I was, I still strove to make our impossible marriage work. Those were hard times. But nothing compared to what Butch dished out after his father passed away. That's when he started to beat me."

Logan sensed that these words may have never been spoken out loud.

"Leanne Capshaw was my best friend, and the only person who saw the black eyes and cuts and bruises. When Butch fractured my collarbone, Leanne made me a sling to hold my arm still so it could heal without me going to the hospital. The irony of a friendship between the wives of the most corrupt and most upstanding men in Barwell was not lost on either of us, but we never spoke of it. That man painted himself to be a devastated martyr all over town while at home he manipulated and threatened and abused me. I fought an invisible battle every single day, protecting him with my silence."

Logan had stopped trying to break himself out of his ties

156

without her noticing. He was weak with compassion for her. This woman, hard as nails in her black pumps and her clipped language, had been carrying these ugly secrets around with her for twenty-five years. "Tell me about Butch's father," he mustered, hoping to not blow this surreal exclusive.

"Oh everyone hated him. His encounters with the law always ended with him sidling out of the sheriff's office with a leaky grin, to the town's dismay. There was even a complaint filed against the sheriff's office for aiding and abetting a criminal, but the officials were helpless. They issued a statement that there wasn't any evidence to support the accusations brought against Mr. Underwood. He got away with everything. Moses Underwood was an ugly, wretched man, but he was smart. When Thomas Capshaw finally caught him red handed in a drug heist, he took his own life, too proud to face justice. Unfortunately, his son was the one who found him; his treacherous brain spilled all over his desk. That was when Bill Underwood became Butch, the monster, and he escalated to more than just a drug user or petty dealer... he took over as the kingpin."

"Butch and Sheriff Capshaw were immediately enemies. Butch was out for revenge, and Capshaw was equally committed to ending the Underwood dynasty. The life of a sheriff is always dangerous, and Capshaw had put an emergency evacuation plan into place years earlier — just in case. There were a handful of people in town he knew he could trust: Ron Mitchell, the Chief of Police, Darius Burns who owned the Inn..."

"Wait a minute, Ron Mitchell was playing for the law? He was the one pointing a gun at me for asking a question! Isn't his gas station part of Butch's underground system?"

"Mitch is a smart man. He kept his friends close and his enemies closer. He was the one who tipped off Capshaw when he noticed Butch's goons hauling crates into the abandoned warehouse behind his gas station. He was also the one who encouraged Butch a few months earlier to consolidate his operations under one roof – a dilapidated roof that Mitch just happened to own. Underwood's enterprise started with a few shanties in the woods, but it grew into a huge operation once Butch took over. When it started scooping up some of Barwell's best and brightest kids in it's dragnet, Capshaw didn't back down a bit. He dug his heels in even deeper and braced for a fight.

"The official transcript recorded that Sheriff Capshaw answered an emergency call at the Underwood's address on May 30, 1988. What really happened is this…"

Logan's entire body broke out in goose bumps, again.

"Janet, the Sheriff's older sister, lived across the street from Butch and me, and she placed the call because she could hear him brawling with me in the middle of the night. The Sheriff showed up blazing mad because he had just raided an empty meth lab way out in the woods, and now had to confront Butch again face to face. He was sick of dealing with this heinous man caught up in another heinous act. Butch fired on the Sheriff, but Capshaw landed a bullet in his shoulder and disarmed him. The Sheriff didn't underestimate the situation, but he did underestimate Butch. Sheriff Capshaw saved my life that night. He sent me across the street to his own sister's house and called for backup with Butch at gunpoint. But Butch was leaking more poison than blood, threatening Capshaw personally and his idyllic family. When the reinforcements came, the Sheriff slipped away, went home and collected his wife and kid, and just left town. He would have nailed Butch to the wall and put him in jail for life, but Butch escalated things by getting the cops called on him for beating me within an inch of my life." She flinched at the memory. "When everything went up in flames they adjusted their plan so the Capshaw family could escape. Mitch staged a fatal car accident so Butch would never really know whether Thomas and his family were dead or alive. And if they were alive, there would be no way for him to find out where they went. All at a moment's notice, he changed the course of his life to keep them safe." The woman relaying this long kept secret paused and stared at the floor. "Capshaw too. He took no chances. Family was everything to him."

Logan was too shocked to speak. Michelle Claridge was a firsthand witness to the very story he had come all this way to cover. Like gears in a broken timepiece, the wheels in his brain began to turn... clicking, grinding, but still struggling to connect. *What is she getting at?*

A professional, third-party tone returned to her voice. "When he went to jail for domestic assault, which was all he got charged for, I quietly filed for separation while he served out his short sentence, and I got out of town. Once I had a little distance from the situation, I realized how tough I had become, and I couldn't live with myself knowing he won that battle, and he got off scot-free. I couldn't let him run my best friend off a bridge and get away with it. I put myself through law school, came *back* to Barwell, and got myself elected as the District Attorney in the same town my filthy ex-husband lived. All to make sure he could *never* get away with anything, ever again."

She was silent, letting the freight train of understanding rush through the room. She had been playing a classified game of chess with her despicable husband the whole time. He knew she had the legal clout to put him away for good, and she knew he wouldn't hesitate to end her if given the chance. The D.A. paused and made eye contact with Logan. He silently prayed for physical and mental endurance. He had no idea how long he had been tied to this bed, but he was running out of time before he would need to use a restroom. He willed himself to find the capacity to hold it and kept his expression blank.

"Can I ask a question?" He wondered, trying not to appear too eager. He felt after all she had been through that she at least deserved some manners. She nodded. "Why does my chest hurt so bad?"

"You're hurting because you aren't dead," she answered cryptically, loosening his arm from the bindings.

He quickly rummaged through his scattered memories of the past few days until the haze began to clear.

"While you were knocked out in your cell, we armed you with a bulletproof vest. I knew if Butch got a shot at you, he would take it, and honestly we hoped he would so we could arrest him. I was counting on his pride to make him think he could get away with firing in broad daylight. He would get caught, no loopholes. I had a lightweight vest put on you under your jumpsuit. The guard was just supposed to drug you so you wouldn't know you were wearing it, but I guess smashing your head into the wall worked just as good."

Logan reached up and touched the back of his head. A large knot was protruding from his skull.

"Sorry about that," she conceded.

That's why I couldn't get up from the cell, Logan realized. *I was drugged and weighted*. He didn't recall the gunshot. A stream of urgent but incoherent questions strung up Logan's thoughts. He tried to pin down the next one to ask as an analog wall clock ticked awkwardly in the quiet room.

He chose a loose ceiling tile to focus on and decided to waste no time assuming she was aware of everything he could come up with to ask. "The court house records room," he began. "Was I drugged there?"

"No," Claridge said simply. "Missy altered your coffee at the Silver Diner."

Logan stole a glance at her, astonished. She did not look back, and he returned to scrutinizing his ceiling tile. "Is your secretary the same Janet as Capshaw's sister?" he asked, taking a long shot.

"Yes. I kept her as close to me as possible for her

protection from Butch."

"If he is such an evil criminal, why would he want a kid so bad? I would think that a man that selfish and corrupt wouldn't want anything to do with a child." Logan tried to speak delicately, knowing this subject held a lifetime of hurt for the lady in this dismal room.

"All he cared about was his own machismo. The more he got away with, the more he felt like he ruled the world. He was a powerful man, and that type of personality needs to be worshiped. It wasn't about the child... it was about his own twisted ideal of being whatever he needed to be in order to have his reputation upheld as a man not to be challenged. In his own head, he thought he was unconquerable. And I, unfortunately and through no fault of my own, shut him down at the one thing he couldn't force to happen. A toxic person doesn't need much to attach themselves to and poison. For him, it was our baby." Her face belied her sadness as she expressed things that had likely never been put to words.

Logan digested this supply of information. A profound sense of authenticity weighed heavy in the room, the truth being more unlikely than the most creative of lies. "The paper with my name on it... Who placed it in my suitcase and where did it come from?"

The D.A. sized him up, then looked away. She cleared her throat nervously and seemed to be formulating her next statement. The third time she opened her mouth to speak, she finally said, "When is your birthday, Logan?" That was the first time she had called him by his first name.

"July 26th."

"What year?"

"1985."

"Do you have a birth certificate?"

Logan halted. Twenty seconds choked past. "No I do not."

"Why not?"

"Because my parents lost everything in a fire when I was young."

"How old were you?"

"They said I was almost three, but I don't remember it."

She finally looked at him again. "Are you sure there was a fire?" Logan just squinted back at her.

"How did you know I was coming? And more importantly, why did you care that I was coming here?"

After a moment, she answered, but her voice was barely a whisper. "The difference between the truth and a lie is in the details," she quavered.

A fuzzy memory took shape in Logan's mind. A teddy bear. Threadbare and tattered, with stuffing beginning to spill from its neck. A black truck spinning its wheels and rocking sharply, scaring him. Then a strange city with gruff neighbors and a new teddy bear. His father, all along, chiding his inner need to venture forth and conquer, but from a discreet attempt to protect, not inhibit. Never a little league game, never a local band performance. It was all too public. Many silent heartbreaks and lost signals. The high school years of battling constraint and conformism, to no avail, and eventually the struck down notion that marriage would change the roles.

Logan snapped back to the present with a jolt. For the first time, disbelief loosened its noose from around Logan's throat. Gently, the answers clicked. A silent bomb of pure stupefaction let loose through his nerves and a tear of awe escaped down one cheek.

"Capshaw?" he asked.

"Yes," she trembled.

"So, you knew my mother?"

Michelle Claridge started to cry. She nodded.

"My dad... my dad was a police officer?"

"The best."

"He always told me, 'family comes first.' "

" 'Loyalty over ambition.' "

"Oh my god," Logan faltered, staring up at the ceiling.

The D.A. wiped her nose and eyes, and began mercifully untying the rest of his restraints. As soon as he could sit up, Logan gave her the most heartfelt embrace he could manage. All her posturing and moxy had drained away, and she held him like a long lost son. He reeled at the thought that he had considered her his mortal enemy just moments ago. They both breathed a sigh of relief, exhausted from the transparency.

"Do you have any other questions?" she asked.

Logan closed his eyes. "Yes. Can I use a restroom?"

CHAPTER TWELVE

$\mathcal{T}$he labor and delivery ward of the Ruth Willis General Hospital in Linsey, VA hummed with silly joy. Stork balloons and vases of flowers were coming and going, some being delivered and others being taken home. It was a busy day for having babies, but the nurses on staff lived for the rare occasion that would land more than one infant in their arms over the span of a night.

Each of the six hospital suites were occupied today with exhausted mothers and tiny newborns. The young women working as medical assistants bustled back and forth, attending their patients and cooing over them all. A feeble but determined cry could be heard at all times coming from one room or another, and the head nurse went about her duties with a dreamy smile, channeling the sunny color of the walls and doting on her charges like a fairy godmother.

Sadie, despite knowing nothing about where her husband was, had bravely withstood the many questions that presented themselves once the anesthesia wore off from her operation.

When she first held her little son, there was only Francis nearby to smile at or take pictures. With the turmoil of late, she and her husband had never officially agreed on a name, and she had been given no choice but to name him herself. His birth certificate read Josiah David Anders, taking his father's middle name and truthfully his eyes too. She wept at the sight of him, not just for the miracle of birth, but the devastation of being alone to witness it.

Repeatedly explaining to a stream of physicians that the baby's father was detained in a police investigation was not the way Sadie Anders had imagined she would spend her son's first day in the world. Francis had tried to help, but by the seventh exchange Sadie was finally able to speak of it without a tremor in her voice. She knew as soon as the nurses left her room they were trading scandalous expressions of "Poor baby" and "Can you believe it?" There was nothing she could do but let them gossip. As hard as she had fought emotionally throughout her pregnancy, having her perfect childbirth experience be tainted with intrigue and loneliness had not left Sadie unscarred. She hoped she would hear something about Logan by the next day, and tried to busy herself with this new continuum of diapers, feeding schedules, and abstract kisses.

"Mrs. Anders?" a new doctor inquired as he popped his head in the door after rapping twice.

Sadie had finally been sleeping while Francis had gone in search of coffee, but she opened her weary eyes and managed an exhausted "Yes."

The doctor walked over to the bassinet and stopped, looking over the sleeping infant. He didn't poke, or measure, or examine, he just observed. When no noise or comments were heard, Sadie opened her eyes again. "What's wrong, doctor?" she asked, concerned.

He did not reply or acknowledge her, nor did he move. Sadie felt nervous and reached for the nurses' bell.

"Don't," the young doctor said softly.

Sadie put her hand back in her lap and said, "What can I do for you, sir? You haven't introduced yourself."

The physician nodded, his arms crossed, and finally let his gaze leave the patient and fix itself on its mother. It was Logan.

"Oh! Oh Logan!" she cried, her voice catching with surprise.

"Hi, babe," he smiled. He never lost his swagger. He crossed the room and sat next to his wife, sliding his arms behind her in the bed, kissing her face, and holding her close. "Oh sweetheart, our baby... he's perfect," he told her. She was already crying into his shoulder.

As Logan embraced his wife, his eyes lingered on his son until a feeling of peace began to anesthetize the hurts from the past. The gravity of fatherhood descended on him in a raw and wondrous way, and he suddenly missed his parents so bad it ached.

In that moment, Logan also became painfully aware of the

gulf that had grown between him and his wife. A great many things settled and shifted inside him, and he was newly ready for the humility and honesty he had long been avoiding.

"Babe, I know it's been a tough year," he admitted unspecifically. "I want you to know I'm sorry for not being there for you the way I should have been."

Sadie composed herself, although it took a few moments. Tired women are always emotional. "No, Logan, you haven't been there for me," she agreed, darkening. "I needed you, and you pushed me away."

"I know, and you've been a champion support to me. I know I have been difficult to deal with lately. But Sadie... really and truly, I want the old Logan and Sadie back. If you can forgive me, babe... I promise things will be different." He paused, getting no response from her. "Can we start over?"

Sadie looked away. It was a lot to let go of, and she had thought for some time now that things may never be the same again between her and her husband. Her first instinct was to resist, to cling to the painful memories and to extend no grace to him for his mistakes.

As his question hung in the air, she saw out the open door to the hallway where another new mother was resting in a wheelchair. She sat in her robe and slippers next to her husband who held their new baby. The woman stood and stepped over to him, gently tugged his chin away from the child until he looked her in the eyes, and she kissed his lips. Then she smiled, turned, and sat back down.

Several moments of enlightenment dawned on Sadie, and a layer of calm crept gently over her. She couldn't identify what shape it took, sort of like the flashes you see out of your peripheral vision that dart away when you try to look right at them. She stared at the oblivious couple whose private exchange had sent lightning bolts through her and burned all the misgivings away, and suddenly she knew how to forgive Logan.

All she had to do was *choose*.

She turned to her husband with solemnity, and he peered back with an impossible mix of worry and hope. In a tone that foretold she was about to say something polarizing, she spoke clearly and calmly. "Logan?"

His voice broke with nerve. "Yes, yes."

She pursed her lips and then said, "Logan, you are a good man." He didn't know what to say, his expression of anxiety telling all. "You are not perfect. You have made mistakes, and you haven't kept all your promises. But there is not a day I want to live without you next to me, issues and all." Logan looked at the floor and cracked a smile of relief. "I want us to be a family and I hope you are ready for that because we don't have a choice for one thing," she added, glancing in the direction of the crib. "But for another, I just, I... I still believe in our dreams, and I still believe in us."

Logan's eyes closed over balmy tears. And just like that, in an ordinary, unglamorous moment, all the loneliness, the distance, the uncertainty, it all became unimportant. Laying aside the mistakes, the unmet expectations, and bygone errors left a purifying sense of renewal draped between them as they sat together. They each pondered in their own minds this new beginning and the possibilities it brought with it for a fresh sense of contentment. They reached for each other at the same moment, further sealing the special bond between two people who have been through something harrowing together, and survived.

Change happened quickly. New visions of the future emerged as they talked in the hospital room, clearer than ever and beckoning to them to follow along and create a new outcome than the one they had feared only minutes ago. For Logan and Sadie, the future mattered again, and the past was healed and shut tight from the pestilence that had long been scratching at its door.

After meeting at the press frenzy following Bill Underwood's arrest, Cole Hawkinson and Missy Plunkett very quickly shared a transcendent connection of one who possessed the sensibility of making delicious biscuits and the other having a great appreciation for consuming them. Soul mates always have something profound in common, and while butter and flour may not seem to be the most stable of foundations upon which to build love and marriage, it was seemingly enough for these two.

Garrett Graves had refused to set his feet on the Barwell Inn property. Logan's account of the accommodations had caused him to seek refuge at the nearby manor house inn called

Grey Haven, a handsome estate on a high hill with a drive flanked by two stone lions at the road. The only other overnight arrangements for 80 miles were near the river rapids in a trailer-park-camp-ground of sorts, Gwynn Ford Landing, a tidy row of retired yellow school buses converted into overnight suites for tourists seeking a truly unique experience. Strauss chose this as a perfect place to stay and chain smoke himself into early retirement.

Although a detachment of Chronicle staff had been sent out to Virginia to cover all the peripheral stories that would certainly materialize with such a sensational piece of news history coming to pass, Alexis was furiously trapped back at the office. Of course she felt entitled to come along, having done all of the research and grunt work behind the scenes. She thundered around the 18th floor in a terrible temper, muttering awful things in Spanish under her breath, making the other interns terminally miserable.

Francis had returned to Chicago, and Logan and Sadie had accepted the hospitality of Ron Mitchel. His children were grown and his wife had passed long ago, and his big farm house was roomy and peaceful. Logan had gladly agreed to stay with Mitch, and relished the chance to get to know one of his father's closest friends who had surely helped save his life more times than anyone probably knew. Until Logan had interviewed every last prospect, witness, and neighbor, he wasn't going home anyway. His first article covering the Capshaw case was already released on the internet, and the Chronicle back home had his headlines crowning their front pages.

'UNSOLVABLE MYSTERY' OF SHERIFF CAPSHAW: SOLVED!!

GRAND CENTRAL STATION OF METH LABS FOUND IN RURAL VIRGINIA

FAMILY FOUND LIVING IN HIDING AFTER 25 YEARS PRESUMED DEAD

COUNTRY SHERIFF FINALLY PUTS WORST ENEMY BEHIND BARS

The Windy City buzzed with the pride that one of their own had ripped from obscurity such a ruthless criminal and proportionately upstanding justice-keeper in one fell swoop. Social media sites were trending **#clarkkentlogananders**, **#capshawcase** and **#supermanisreal** as the public relished the 'newsman turned superhero' nature of the story. Many other reporters were writing their own articles about the guy writing the Capshaw articles. The unthinkable odds of a stranger showing up in a faraway town and slamming the truth into the open had caused the whole thing to catapult itself into a miniature, semi-national media frenzy.

Despite word spreading like brushfire and every neighboring county sending teams of local reporters to Barwell to get the scoop, Logan had managed to keep his personal connection to Butch Underwood out of the papers. He knew at any moment it could come to light, but those who knew the truth were still maintaining the circle of trust and not making mention of it. The pressure was exhilarating and unnerving. Logan was reeling with the heady responsibility of delivering nationwide breaking news, the novelty of fatherhood, and the personal debt he owed to the people who had been looking out for him over the last few days of tremendous stress and danger.

It was Saturday morning when Sadie and baby Josiah were finally discharged from the hospital. Both she and Logan were relieved to not have to travel all the way home with a newborn right away. But they were also equally nervous about leaving the hospital with their five-day-old little boy strapped into a borrowed car seat, wearing only a blue onesie purchased from Dollar General. Fortunately, a tiny group of ladies from the knitting club at Barwell Baptist Church came to visit just in time to make sure Logan's son didn't catch a cold. With all the hospitality in the South, they presented the little Anders' family with a red and blue crocheted blanket, a fleece hat and a jacket for the baby boy. The hat was large enough to fit a two-year-old's head and the jacket was misshapen beyond usage, but that made them even more colloquially charming. Logan and Sadie tucked the hat and jacket safely away as tokens of this unmistakably wild birth story, then wrapped their little boy in his new, warm quilt as they exited the Labor and Delivery Ward at Willis General.

They rode silently for the hour-long drive to Mitch's farm. They took turns peering into the back seat of the black rental car to make sure the baby was okay and then smiling, exhaustedly, at each other.

*   *   *

Ron Mitchel's big gray clapboard farm house stood in the

middle of a huge field, attended only by a tall silver silo, a pen of hounds, and a cluster of mismatched trees. For acres in every direction there was nothing but soybean fields, and the distant tree lines were the only neighbors. The drive to Barwell took a full fifteen minutes... maybe less if you were driving something newer than the pickup truck that was getting to the age where it would accelerate when it darn well pleased.

The Mitchel farm was less than three miles south of the Miners Gap Bridge, and beyond the trees to the West, deep in the woods, were the long- abandoned and charred remains of a meth lab. Mitchel's property was bordered on the West and South by dense forests, on the North by the state route, and on the East by the Carrollton River. No one stumbled upon a farm or anything for that matter this far away from town; the only folks who visited this neck of the woods came on purpose.

The normally tomb-like farm house was lively and full of people. The posse who had protected and risked so much for Logan during his investigation were all gathered together under the Mitchel roof for a tenuous but much anticipated visit, and since dozens of unexpected twists of fate had occurred amongst them all, the tension quickly gave way to genuine care and a deep familial tie.

The yard was full of cars, and two matted long-haired cats wound their way warily between them all, as cats have a need to survey and approve of all that trespasses on their property. Lengths of twine were hung between the trees, with dried gourds hanging from them like party lights. The front porch was jumbled with fishing poles and extra coolers, as well as the curious remains of an elaborate pool flotation device. Neither the child nor the location for which it was intended to be used were anywhere nearby. Quite a few things seemed to have made their way on to the porch and never left.

Inside the great pine door with the black iron latch assembly, the walls were shrouded with aging wallpaper in a soothing shade of soft earthen red, an unmatchable color all it's own. Past the central stairs several large rooms led off the hall; each a different murky shade of gold, persimmon, and sage, the colors of autumn outside. The old, dusty drapes made each room feel timeless and calm. Framed pictures on the walls in every stage of the evolution of photography from genuine turn-of-the-century sepia to sharp modern color hinted at the many decades this house had stood.

Everyone had been too noisy and stayed indoors all day to notice the sky was gray with an oncoming storm. Logan and Sadie were taking in the culture of this new family, and although they were unaccustomed to this kind of Southern warmth, being stout Chicagoans themselves, they had tilted their barriers out of the way and let them all rush into their hearts.

"You know, this would be even better if it were wrapped in bacon!" Daniel Burns was exclaiming, holding up a skewer of marinated beef to show Logan. "We could call it a meat-cicle." He grinned with pride, and Missy pummeled his arm cheerfully. Daniel's smile was much more relaxed now that he wasn't nervously protecting an oblivious family member from an old grudge.

"I'm sure nothing could improve upon Missy's filet tips," Logan assured, slipping an arm around his cousin's shoulder and punctuating his statement with a kiss on her head. She beamed at him but shooed them both out of the way so she could make her way into the living room.

Michelle Claridge and Missy filled the table with copious amounts of food from the kitchen and poured drinks from an array of dispensers on the buffet. Leland was setting up the chessboard for anyone who dared to challenge him after dinner. Ron Mitchel snoozed contentedly by the fire with the TV turned down low on a western show. Some of Logan's favorite upbeat jazz music rambled in the background, and Daniel was sampling everything that came off the grill, out of the fridge, or from the oven. His wrists were pink from being smacked.

Thunder roiled through the midafternoon sky. Steely clouds were amassing on the horizon and making their way across the wide Carrollton River like the armies of ancient Egypt, immense and far flung. A gash of lightning severed the sky in two with an accompanying crack of thunder, which startled little baby Josiah from his sleep. His cherubic face rumpled with angst.

"It's okay," Sadie purred to her son, her hand behind his downy head. "It's okay. It's just a storm."

Logan walked into the room and wrapped his two favorite people in his arms. He ached with *rightness*. Though his little boy mewed with displeasure, Logan lifted him off of his mother's chest and folded him in so close he could feel Josiah's tiny heart beat.

"Look at that angel," Janet cooed. The elderly are always so in tune with babies, maybe because of their acute sense of the circle of life that they are closing in on, and the little ones who are just embarking on it. "He looks like his daddy," she winked.

"Do you think so?" Logan replied, transparent with hope. He secretly wished his son would take after him, but maybe with more athletic ability. "I think he has my nose," he added sheepishly.

"Son, he's got everything he needs," the old woman said broadly, knowing what he really meant. Logan didn't mind her calling him 'son.'

A lazy hour passed as this newly mended family offered each other uninitiated stories of the past, a hand with the oven door or the pot holder, and glasses of tea, thick with real sugar. The peaceful country afternoon in and of itself carefully and tediously bathed the wounds of the cold war they had all just fought together, like a battlefield medic. A shared trauma has a way of knitting people together in a way no other experience can manage, the payoff being in direct proportion to the risk.

Logan learned many things about who his parents really were. Each person, except Missy who was too young to know, volunteered shards of memories that Logan silently clicked together to try and rebuild an accurate picture of the people he called Mom and Dad. He was good natured about the influx of behind the scenes details, but the more he found out, the more a nagging discomfort began to whir in the back of his mind, bringing up the inappropriate fact that he had been lied to his whole life.

"We need to finish up with the grill," Sadie said, looking out at the weather. "It's going to rain soon."

"At least everyone is here and we have plenty of candles and blankets in case we end up losing power."

"Oh Logan, you don't think we will, do you?!"

"Babe, it will be fine. It will be an adventure," Logan smiled.

Sadie swatted at his arm. "Just go look in the basement, will you? Mitch said they were down there, but just make sure," she requested, finishing her iced tea and rising gingerly from the couch to fill her glass again.

Logan started down the stairs with Josiah nestling into his neck as the doorbell rang, and Sadie changed directions and headed for the door.

Logan reached the bottom of the steps and fished around for the overhead light. *Everyone is here,* he thought. *Who in the world could that be?*

Sadie's glass crashed above his head from the ground level.

Racing back up the stairs holding his son like a football, he saw his wife standing with the door half open, her hand over her mouth, looking ashen. The house guests were suddenly silent, and Josiah instinctively pressed himself into his father's jugular.

The jazz music seemed to falter and lilt. When no one moved, Logan walked to the door and pulled it the rest of the way open. He stopped breathing and stepped aside as his parents entered the house.

CHAPTER THIRTEEN

*T*homas and Leanne Capshaw held each other in a hushed and emotional embrace with their son. Logan was rigid with shock, anger, relief and a barbaric sense of distrust. Michelle, Leland, Missy and Daniel had come to see who was at the door and stood stunned beyond words, peering at them from the various doorways. Logan's parents shifted and cried some more at the sight of their grandson. Poor Sadie, hormonal and exhausted, just sobbed without reservation at first sight of her beloved in-laws, and the spectacle of them holding her child was unsurpassable.

As the Capshaw's fervently greeted each person - and the shock and speechless weeping began to subside - Janet came shuffling down the hallway. Oblivious without her hearing aid, she nearly fainted at the sight of her brother standing before her.

"Oh my lands," she cried softly, and her frail hand flew to

her mouth as she swayed backward.

"Easy does it," Daniel managed, taking her gently by the shoulders to steady her.

"Oh, darlin'... oh, Tommy," she croaked, collapsing into tears and gripping her brother around the waist. Everyone else started crying all over again.

Logan and Sadie looked at each other. They read each others thoughts; there was no way this was possible but they were both seeing the same thing, so it must be real.

"Is she related to your dad?" Sadie questioned, confused.

"She's my aunt," Logan explained, realizing his wife knew very little of the back story he had learned. She had been preoccupied with the baby and was still catching up on all she had missed. Another wave of understanding and appreciation for this densely meaningful reunion came over her, and she just whimpered and nodded.

"Good God!" Mitch yawped from the living room. Thomas had slipped in and shaken him awake, and the two men hugged like veterans of war.

The whole brood began to return to the preparations they were making before the doorbell rang, amidst murmurings of "What is going on?" and "Am I really seeing this?" Each person took their chance to hug the necks of the two people that brought them all together in each other's lives and, strangely, under this roof.

As everyone scooted the table settings around to make room for Thomas and Leanne, the questions finally started spilling out. Mitch just paced the kitchen for lack of ability to relax at the presentation of long lost friends who had twice been falsely presumed dead.

"You mean the car blew up?!" Michelle was exclaiming, still dabbing urgent tears from her eyes.

"It knocked me on my back," Logan relayed, his own eyes refusing to stay dry. He nodded toward his dad. "How on earth did you survive?" He had uttered the crucial question.

Thomas had spoken very little. He released his sister Janet from his side, where she had been since he had returned baby Josiah to his mother, and he placed both hands on the back of the chair his wife was seated in.

"When we pulled up to the curb, we were suddenly and quite roughly pulled out of our car and shoved into a waiting hand cab. Immediately, the truck slammed into our vehicle and staged our death." No one could believe what they were hearing. "We were held at gunpoint, so we didn't run, but when we got out of the city, our kidnapper turned out to be a witness protection officer. He had been instructed to return us to obscurity until things blew over."

Thomas looked slowly around the room, visually landing on every face present. "Those of you in this room are the only people who knew our alias. Michelle is the only one who knew how to contact us. When she told us that inquiries were being made about the Capshaw case, I started to worry that even the slightest attention might trigger Underwood's radar, and then he could potentially trace us back to Chicago. I knew someone was digging into the old story, but I had no idea it was Logan." He shook his head. "Michelle warned me about the possibility of having to go underground again, but planning a funeral was not what I was expecting." He himself hardly seemed to believe he was telling this story. "Butch would have found out where we were before long. And he would have killed me himself. Truthfully when we were shoved into that hand cab, I thought Butch was having us kidnapped."

"Did he think you were going to show up in Barwell?" Logan asked his father.

"I'm sure everyone was shocked to see a man your age instead of me," Thomas mused, shaking his head again. "But I had to play dead."

"So," Daniel said slowly, "If you weren't dead... where were you?" Everyone in the room turned to hear the answer.

"We just went home," Leanne said. "No one was looking for us, so we stayed there until Shelby called and said it was safe." She shrugged her shoulders as if it were the most normal thing in the world to falsify your own demise, and then return home to watch your favorite 8 o'clock television show.

"Who is Shelby?" Sadie asked, wide eyed, feeling left out of the loop again.

Michelle leaned over and laid her head on Leanne's shoulder. "It's me," she smiled. "Leanne gave me the nickname in high school. No one has called me Shelby in… so many years." She choked on the memory and squeezed her friend's shoulder, almost as if to make sure she was really there.

Everyone was so wrapped up in hearing from Thomas and Leanne that Logan stepped out back unnoticed. He was wiped out from the emotional ping-pong of having everything he thought had ever been true, past and present, turned upside down and shaken to bits. Although his initial reaction had been ceremoniously joyful at seeing his parents, the longer he listened to them relay the twists and turns of the last few weeks, the more restless he became. The chip on his shoulder had only grown as he learned more and more how distant he truly had been from the truth about himself and his family. This was all too much to process; he had finally reached his limit of surprises.

Logan slipped back through the house and tugged on a jacket. Missy noticed from the hallway. "Where are you going?" she whispered, seeing him perch sunglasses on his head and unhook his car keys from their peg.

"Just need some air," he answered with unmasked annoyance, and walked out the front door with no further attempt at civility. He crunched across the gravel drive and spat at the cats to make them run away, and tumbled into his rental car full of tension. He let the car idle while he tried to decide where to go. He looked up when his father tapped on the window.

"You okay, Logan?"

"Yeah dad," he sighed, rolling his eyes.

"I know this is a lot to handle, son." He looked away, trying to land on a way to bridge the gap. "Can I ride with you to wherever you're going?"

"Sure," Logan said gritting his teeth. Thomas slipped into the passenger seat, and the tension mounted as Logan backed the car up and steered it toward the road, with no destination in mind.

Thomas was quiet. Logan was quieter. The car seemed to want to drive toward the mountains, so Logan cooperated.

"Son, I want to show you something. Turn left at the next road." Logan glanced at his dad in the passenger seat, still a little spun up and unsure that he wasn't just seeing a ghost. He turned left and silently followed his father's directions, quite possibly for the first time in his life. They pulled slowly into a clearing in the trees and onto another road flanked by widely spread houses with seasonal flags hanging from their banisters and pinwheels in the yard. Logan was instructed to turn again, this time down a dirt road that passed a residence facing the state route and looked as if it went straight through the mountains.

Sure enough, the road began to climb over the foothills of the Blue Ridge Mountains. At Thomas's direction, the black sedan slowed at the end of a short driveway nestled along the mountains where the old house stood that Logan had discovered on foot the week before. Logan parked the car and looked at his father questioningly, still wordless. His dad just looked through the windshield with past decades in his eyes. Finally and with a tremor, he said, "This was our home, Logan."

He had already known. He guessed as they drove that he was being taken to either the meth lab or the Capshaw residence. A memory or two began to shine through the overgrowth and dust.

A tingle ran through Logan as he and his dad got out of the car and walked toward the abandoned house. He had the feeling that he was about to be ambushed for some reason, but he choked it out and replaced it with some abstract form of logic that made him feel somehow in control.

"Dad, watch out. There's a hornet's nest right there in the eaves."

Thomas nodded but continued to carefully climb the steps to the porch, keeping an eye on the mummified hostel of hornets. Several of them were flying around, with their incessant sinister buzzing. The constant buzz of a hornet could be used to invoke terror and madness, like Chinese water torture. Logan remembered his meeting with Judge Hawthorne and shuddered.

Thomas showed Logan around the dilapidated homestead he had lived in as a toddler. He patiently let his father relive their life here, and told him about the experience he had sleeping in the barn in the very truck that had gone over the bridge. The bricks began to topple between them, and the irony and magic of all that had happened began to soothe them both from the wounds of the past.

Pangs of thunder crashed outside. Logan walked to the kitchen window and felt drawn to the barn out back. He exchanged glances with his dad, who seemed to read his mind, and the two walked out the back door and hopped to the ground as the wind shook the sky with threats of dismemberment.

Instinctively, Thomas led his son around the barn, not through it, and slowed when he came in view of the grand vista of the Carrollton River at its widest girth. Logan gazed for a long time at the clouds occupying the sky, billowing their reflection on the water. This was the scene from his memories.

"Do you remember that time when…"

"Of course, Logan."

"Why did you take me inside?"

"Why wouldn't I? It wasn't safe."

"I didn't want safe."

"You were three. You were my responsibility. Everything I've ever done was to protect you."

"That's a loaded statement."

The two men continued to avoid eye contact and studied the sky, standing in the wild open. Logan's cell phone warbled in his pocket. "Yeah," he answered. Thomas looked over at his son and saw he was staring out across the lake, and his breathing was suddenly shallow. "Thanks." Logan pressed the end button on his iPhone and stared at the home screen. Then he folded his arms and a dangerous smile of mischief, manic and satisfied, escaped his lips.

"Who was it, son?"

Logan bit his fist, and finally answered, "Sheriff Crutcher is allowing me to interview Butch Underwood."

"I'm not sayin' anything to no reporter," Butch swore, leaning back in the aluminum chair he was squatting on.

"You don't have to tell me anything," Logan responded pleasantly.

"Then why are you here?" Butch leaned back in his chair with impenetrable rebellion.

Logan checked his watch. "Because you tried to kill me," he said, placing the ball firmly in his own court.

"Well, nosy reporters are better off dead," Butch countered, remorseless.

"Why is that? I can only assume that's the case because you have something to hide."

"Nah, Underwoods just know how to run this town better'n the powers that be." His pride in his despicable family was genuine.

"Is that so?"

"Yeah, it is."

"Are you admitting you killed the Capshaw family?"

Butch sneered. "Didn't have to. He went off that bridge because he had it comin' to him.

"Uh, why is that?"

The incarcerated man sat the front legs of his chair down again. "That sheriff went outside his jurisdiction to arrest my dad," he snapped. "He would have never been convicted if he hadn't... if he had lived." A deep sadness flashed in his eyes but evaporated into anger again. "That sheriff got what was comin' to him," he vowed again.

Logan sat back in his chair. With empathy and caution, he focused on the table, trying not to be too provoking. "So because he caused your dad to commit suicide, he deserved to die too?"

Butch was caught off guard by this response. The two men sat without speaking for a few minutes, but strangely, it was not awkward or uncomfortable. It was more like they both needed a moment, and were giving it to each other. Logan had plenty of questions but was determined to listen and learn whatever Butch wanted him to know. Butch broke the silence.

"There was a picture of me and my dad hunting in the

mountains, from my senior year of high school. It was sitting on his desk." He faltered for adequate words, shaking his head softly and looking away. "It was covered in his blood when I found him dead."

Logan nodded and didn't breathe for fear he might huff out this tiny flame of truth that was starting to burn.

"My dad struggled for everything he had. He never got no breaks. That arrogant Sheriff couldn't stand my family makin' a livin' the way we did."

"You manufacture illegal drugs, man," Logan crowed. "Why would you expect the law to approve of that?"

"It don't matter! A man's got to provide and just because my dad did well for himself outside the confines of all the fancy laws, he wadn't a bad man."

Logan forced his eyebrows to keep from rising, but couldn't help a few gratuitous questions. "Didn't he shoot your neighbors house cat because it 'trespassed on his property' and set fire to the Lackey family farm in the next county?"

Butch puckered up his face and simply replied, "All them folks did wrong by my dad and he wadn't doin' anything but defendin' his manhood."

Logan was satisfied that Butch believed he and his father were totally justified in their actions, and the Capshaw family had indeed died in the wreck near the Miners Gap Bridge in 1988. And that was exactly what he was waiting for.

"So when Sheriff Capshaw stole your daddy's pride and he blew his brains out because of it, you decided to exact revenge, right?"

Butch looked at Logan, suddenly transfixed with rage. A stream of threats erupted from his thin lips, in every shade of profanity imaginable. Logan peered around the room non-confrontationally, waiting his turn. When Butch was pleased with himself enough to recline again and cease his vulgarities, Logan turned to the opaque glass and nodded to the observer hidden behind the reflection. He returned his gaze to the hulking, ill tempered convict, and as they locked eyes, Logan flushed with victory. Thomas opened the metal door and stood against the wall, folding his hands.

"You had your chance, Butch. Your Dad lost to my Dad a long time ago, and now you're losing to me."

Butch's gnarled face froze. His eyes swiveled almost imperceptibly between Thomas and his son. Logan didn't move until he saw in Butch's eyes that he understood he was sitting across from the little boy he thought had drowned.

Logan's cell phone rang. Still looking Butch in the face, he answered Alexis's call. Strauss wanted to know when he was getting back to town because now everyone in Chicago-land wanted his star reporter to till up the fallow ground of their own mysteries. "Yeah, I'm leaving tomorrow," he said, gesturing his father to leave the room and he himself following.

"We're done here."

ABOUT THE AUTHORS

Marshal Hunter has been an independent filmmaker and video producer for over 14 years. He is passionate about telling great stories in many forms. Capshaw is his first published novel, which he is extremely excited to share with the world. As much as he loves storytelling, he loves his family more. Hunter has been married 13 years to his beautiful wife, Apollonia. Together, they have three incredible boys who keep life interesting.

Leah Spradlin is an entrepreneur and actress and has been an East Coast Virginia native for all her thirty years. Telling great stories of every size and genre is the only thing she loves more than being entertained by great stories. She has been married to her husband Rob for ten years and they have a son and daughter who bring magic to their world every day. Capshaw is her first published work, and she has many more dreams waiting patiently for their turn to come to life.

CONNECT WITH THE CAPSHAW FAMILY

FOLLOW US ON SOCIAL MEDIA

FACEBOOK.COM / CAPSHAWNOVEL

INSTAGRAM.COM / CAPSHAWNOVEL

#CAPSHAWNOVEL

JOIN OUR MAILING LIST

NOBLEGIANTBOOKS.COM/SUBSCRIBE

Made in the USA
Middletown, DE
18 September 2015